Teresa H Dean

Reveries of a widow

Teresa H Dean

Reveries of a widow

ISBN/EAN: 9783337414351

Printed in Europe, USA, Canada, Australia, Japan

Cover: Foto ©Andreas Hilbeck / pixelio.de

More available books at **www.hansebooks.com**

Reveries of a Widow

BY

TERESA DEAN

NEW YORK
TOWN TOPICS PUBLISHING CO.
1899

To my friend—in trouble, in sorrow, in happiness, in right, in wrong; not always with reason, not always with understanding, but always with that sympathy and never-failing response that make friendship real—my mother.

REVERIES OF A WIDOW

REVERIES OF A WIDOW.

I.

JACK seems to take it as a personal offense that Colonel Bradbury forgave his wife. Jack thinks that he knows men, that he knows women. He is a big fellow, brawny, broad-shouldered, athletic, not young, not old; good-natured, sympathetic, indifferent—just the man for women to rave over. But Jack doesn't know it all. He seems to me to be sort of incomplete. When a man lives to his age and does not marry, you can't help wondering what it is in his life that has chilled his heart into facts. He declares that he has never been in love. I don't suppose for an instant that he tells all those other women that he has never loved. He is frank with me, probably because he knows all about the two loves of mine.

.　　.　　.　　.　　.　　.

That was an amusing thing—that white-haired, handsome elderly maiden saying to me: "A widow?" Then she looked at my dress questioningly—an organdie over a joyous rose taffeta—and added, hesitatingly and apologetically, " g-r-a-ss ? "

" Yes, grass, and under the grass," I said.

She was naturally shocked, but she finally accepted the situation—or me—and said :

" A widow twice, and so young ; twice married, and there are some who never marry at all and never have the opportunity."

The little that she added about the lives of some women being so full, too full of duties to others to allow them to think of love and marriage, hinted at volumes of pathos ; but I don't think that duty to others has prevented Jack from marrying—unless it is the so-called duty to honor and social laws that has kept him from skipping away with some other man's wife. I would not say it to any one but myself—Jack is a good fellow, but his dearest friends always seem to be beyond his reach, because of the husband in the background.

He was from the first very much interested in the Bradbury-Ward elopement. Jack's knowing No. 2—Over the Grass—makes him feel at home with me, but the way in which he slapped down the paper, when he read that Colonel Bradbury had forgiven his wife, was a startler. He threw it violently to the floor and said :

"It is an outrage!"

"What is an outrage ?"

"For a husband to forgive a wife that has eloped with another man ; not only forgive her, but go way out to Chicago to meet her, and actually look happy to be with her again. It is an outrage, and it—it encourages crime!"

"In men or in women?" I ask.

. . . . . .

Jack says I have some sense, am comprehensive and have a mind that has broadened into camaraderie, but he didn't like that question. How he glared at me! But one learns—has to learn—a lot of things, and one of them is—to look innocent. He glared and then decided I wanted information, so he answered conservatively :

"In women, of course. How can Colonel Bradbury ever trust his wife again? She will take another skip, see if she doesn't."

"If she does she may again pay him the compliment of returning to him." No mistaking this time that Jack was annoyed.

"Compliment! Bosh!" said he.

It was of no use to argue. After you have been married twice you learn to argue with yourself, but not with a man. I said nothing. Jack would not have it that way.

"Where does the compliment come in?" he demanded.

"By returning to her husband she proved to him how much stronger his hold upon her was than that of the man who had made such desperate, mad love to her."

You learn all that is best and all that is worst in a man with whom you live for several years—marriage is such a leveler of illusions. Even the man who had only tried to fascinate, could not hold the wife! All the time that she was with him, she was thinking of the nobility of the husband and who could and did forgive.

.   .   .   .   .   .

And this husband has in him the blood of the race that never forgives—and never forgets. And those drops of copper-colored blood in Bradbury's veins may have reminded him of a debt he owed. Perhaps—possibly— you never can tell—there may have been times, in the short years of their married life, when he has asked for forgiveness and

got it. He only repaid what he had bor-
rowed.

.   .   .   .   .   .

Jack does not know; in his bachelor life he
has seen but one side of the question. He
may not have really loved, because, in his
experience, he has stood in the way of his
own trust and faith in women. He may have
seen—and he may have caused—faithlessness
in wives; not in open sin but in that end-of-
the-century way of playing with edged tools
—that trifling with what should be held sacred.
He may not be the man to take away a friend's
wife, but he can count several on his list
whom he has comforted in their woes, real or
fancied.

He has comforted them and flattered himself that he has guided them into philosophical
paths of discretion. And these women have
trusted him.

.   .   .   .   .   .

Wives forgive because they are women.
They discover the indiscretion, but can be
made to believe that the line has been drawn
this side of guilt—because they so want to
believe.

A man can believe in his own innocence so

long as there is a loop-hole left for him in
which to find an explanation and be forgiven.

Really in these modern days—I wouldn't
say to anyone but myself—life seems to be
made up of explanations and forgiveness—
explanations from the husband and forgiveness from the wife. You forgive because the
conventions of society demand there be no
scandal. You "believe" because, if there be
no decisive step taken, your own self-respect
demands that you believe; suspicion, even, is
beneath you. You must "believe" if you stay
in "harness"—otherwise you condone, and
lower your own high standard of womanhood.

.   .   .   .   .   .

When Jack and his kind come into your life
they don't really tempt you. It is not often
that you must ask forgiveness; but you do love
to trifle, and the finer sense of honor does
wear off a bit.

It is strange how constant men can be to
the unattainable—constant, loyal and true—if
you hold them "right there," and never allow
a slip over the trifling love-line.

Now, there's Jack. He says that he does
not love me, but that he likes me five hun-
dred times better than any woman he ever

knew; that I am different from most women; that I keep my head and don't go to pieces; that, though I was the innocent victim of the wrong-doing of others, I am not embittered in my nature, and am still trusting, and can even be just to my enemies.

Poor, dear Jack! How little he knows! How little men know of women, anyway! I wonder what Jack would say if I should tell him how much I have learned about making circles fit corners; that the peccadilloes of Over-the-Grass were perfectly well known to me for two years before this last climatic break which all the world came to know, and that I have learned never to rub the fur the wrong way, and never——

I wonder what Jack thinks of Judge Falconer, the Kentuckian, who acquitted the husband who killed his wife's lover. I must find out if he thinks that will encourage crime, too, like Colonel Bradbury's forgiveness.

II.

Jack seems to be a bit wary of me since I defended Colonel Bradbury's forgiveness of his eloping wife. I must be careful. It would never do to let Jack know or allow him to think that I have opinions. Can't afford to lose Jack! Jack is—well, Jack is Jack. I need him. I need him to bat up against, as it were. Those two husbands of mine— Under-the-Grass and Over-the-Grass, respectively—were all right in their way, but their way, as I saw it—on the surface, at least —was too finely shaded. Jack is out-and-out and teaches one pointers, and a woman—wife, widow, or twice a widow—needs pointers— must have them. Pointers make a winner. But my! They keep you watching that the edge of your intellect is keen enough to " cut a hair!"

.   .   .   .   .   .

The keen edge of my intellect must have had a hack in it somewhere when I asked Jack what he thought of the Kentucky Judge who

acquitted the husband for killing his wife's
lover.   Jack answered, thoughtfully and carefully :

"One would have to understand the circumstances thoroughly to be able to express
an opinion."

Come to think of it, perhaps he was not so
wary of me.   It may have been that he was
thinking of other circumstances.   There's no
use denying it—all to myself—there are several " circumstances " in Jack's own bachelor
life.   And I suppose—again to myself—that
there have been occasions when he himself
would have liked to have others lenient and
conservative in opinion until they investigated
" circumstances."

So my little careless, casual question was not
very satisfactorily answered.   I really did not
find out whether he thought this, like the
other, would or would not " encourage crime."
I like Jack better when he is not quite so
careful about expressing opinions.   I like to
have him think he " knows it all " and then
prove to myself how little he knows.

.   .   .   .   .   .

It was amusing about the long enveloping
wrap to go over my bathing suit.   It was cer-

tainly, in one way, the hit of my life. I
knew it would be. Another proof of the mad
desire, in men, for the unattainable. And
this time the " unattainable " was the glimpse
of poor me. It makes me smile. Jack just
patted himself on the back—metaphorically
—when he said, " You must wear a wrap, or
something, this year that will cover you,"
then he added, as if it were a heinous fault of
my own :

" You are naturally so conspicuous with your
blonde hair and your — your — well, your
curves, if I must say it. You always have
every eye upon you, even in street costume—
and it is entirely wrong for you to appear on
the beach in a bathing costume. You remember the annoyance you had last year, don't
you? You must pardon me for speaking so
plainly, but really, with all your experience
as the wife of two men, and both of them
thorough men of the world, you are the most
unsophisticated — unconscious, innocent, or
whatever you will—you need a man to tell
you what to do, and this year you have not a
husband to stand between you and the social
shafts you will run into."

    .   .   .   .   .   .

He said a lot of things.   After a man once gets started he is very much like a woman. He talks.   Jack talked.   He said I must wear a wrap over my bathing suit, and have it come down to my heels and have my maid take it at the very edge of the water.   I chuckled to myself.   I saw fun ahead.   Wraps and maids are all right in some localities on the coast, but where we bathe—Atlantic City—it is un-heard of.   I wonder why?   Philadelphia is so pure-minded, I suppose—um-m-m.   I am sur-rounding myself with a few question marks—being alone.

I got the wrap.   It is just what might have been expected.   I am the most noticed woman on the beach.   Jack says it is respectful ad-miration.   Um-m again!—to myself.   Men are idiots, and Jack—great, big, brawny, ath-letic Jack—the worst of the lot.   He doesn't know it yet.   And he never will.   No man dare say to Jack that it is anything but respect-ful admiration that makes him so interested in the lady who wears the wrap, and ask who she is and—poor Jack!   And he thinks me un-sophisticated!

.   .   .   .   .   .

He is, this time, the victim of himself.   I

am glad of it. It was mean of him to refer, in that way, to my annoyance last year. I was not to blame for that suit of mine shrinking and growing beautifully less each day. Strange how some cloth will grow less from every direction!

Now, that suit of mine, in the beginning, was regular. It was Quaker-like. It was even made in Philadelphia, and it was warranted to stay with me for the season. It did stay with me, but it grew affectionately clinging in the days I waited for Over-the-Grass to come. Over-the-Grass should not have delayed so. I had to bathe each day, and when the suit began to fit something like the suits of the "birds" in "The Whirl of the Town," and the bathers—water-bathers and sand-bathers—began to comment on women who walk well and a few other things, I wanted to purchase another suit—a longer one, a broader one, and one that—well, anyway, another one.

I wanted another one out of respect to the possible opinions of Over-the-Grass. Of course, he was not Over-the-Grass then; all that has happened since. But Jack and the rest said no. They said that Over-the-

Grass was sure to hear that his wife was, or had been, the belle of the billows and beach, and they wanted him to have a full realization of the reason for it. It would do him good. It would punish him, too, for delaying so long in putting in an appearance. On the way down to the coast he overheard a man say that Mrs. —— was the most admired woman on the beach—his own wife!!!

If I were going to write a book on how to make a husband attentive I would recommend a bathing suit that was designed and started in its career with all due deference to modesty. If the salt in the water will interfere and upset well-laid and virtuous plans, a woman cannot be held responsible. Over-the-Grass, Jack, and all the rest never held me responsible, and their open admiration nearly turned my head. It is such a comfort, not to be held responsible for anything of that kind. And you are never held responsible with a handsome husband in the background. Over-the-Grass was — is — handsome. That was—is—the worst of it. Women—but I must not think of all that. That was then; this is now.

.   .   .   .   .   .

But it was free and easy and a good time, all the time, with the husband to take the responsibility. Free and easy—not prudish, not reckless. Just a time without stopping to weigh things, with the scale eternally coming down on the side that is sure to interfere with the pace you have struck, be the pace what it may.

This year I am responsible. I am alone. Over-the-Grass is lost in the shuffle of morals. Hence the wrap. Hence Jack. Jack was there before, of course, but hence his care, anxiety and officiousness, and hence all these men who prefer to take sand-baths near my maid who waits with my wraps for me to come out of the water. I did not have to be careful this year about extreme " modesty " in my bathing suit—that was a comfort both morally and physically. It being destined to be covered with a wrap on the way to the water, I did not have to worry. It is made without unnecessary cloth to get in the way and to get weighted with water. I was only particular about two things—fit and color.

Limited amount of cloth necessitates a good fit, and to my mind there is really no color more unassuming than black. But I expect I am a sort af a silhoutte when my maid takes off and adjusts my wrap. Jack insisted upon having it white. White, he said, was not so conspicuous along the beach in the midst of the lookers-on in their summer costumes.

As the season advances all the suits are shrunk to a close fit, and the bathers all look alike; no one is more conspicuous than another; no one notices as they skip along the beach and pell-mell into the water.

No one is noticed particularly but myself. I am the only woman who wears a wrap!

Poor, dear Jack!

III.

Well! well! well! Of all things! Jack, cautious Jack, bachelor Jack, man-of-the-world Jack—Jack of all men, writing love letters, and to a married woman! I don't know when I have been so taken off my feet. Gracious goodness! if, after all, Jack is going to pan out to be only like other men, what good is he to me? The world is full of men, but there are so few like Jack—as Jack was; yes—was. I will only whisper it to myself, but he does not seem just the same now. Maybe I will get over it.

His greatest charm to me was his masterfulness; his being the rage with men and women, and he, apparently, perfectly unconscious of the raging—just going on in his quiet way, with a look of astonishment if any one ventured over his own boundary line.

.   .   .   .   .   .

Of course women like him, rave, go wild over him. They can't manage him. Like men after the unattainable, they lose their heads because he is not susceptible, or does not succumb to one of their artifices. And with him they actually drop their artifices and their pet rôles, and really show glimpses of the real thing—feeling and heart, particularly if in their hearts there is a grievance. They will even manufacture a grievance, for, of course, sympathy is the weak point, the very weak point, in men like Jack.

Sympathy satisfies to perfection a yearning soul; sympathy is also the rock that blindly bars the door to perdition, until the yearning soul finds itself split into a thousand pieces socially.

.   .   .   .   .   .

And Jack says it was sympathy that made him write those letters! It is very funny. He, to actually pen letters in his own name to a woman who was living with her husband! And here's poor me! When Over-the-Grass got caught in that trap—a woman, "Canadian Club" and sympathy!—Jack's heart just bled for me—is bleeding yet—but letters? Oh, no. He thinks too much of me. He says so. He says in his grand, masterful way:

"I will not write to you. Your trouble is

too new. Your own position is established
on a solid foundation, because you are known
to be a good fellow and a good woman. If,
however, out of the many friends you have
there should be one to come to the front as
particularly interested, the cruel tongue of
scandal would go like wildfire, and the tide
of sympathy, given to you so fully now in
your sorrow, would turn, and even the open
sin of your husband would not protect you."

I had great respect for Jack's caution. If
this open sin of Over-the-Grass could not
protect a woman against the shafts of gossip,
there was nothing in the world that would.

   .   .   .   .   .   .

So, while I felt like "driftwood tossed by
the surging main," I recognized the fact that
pure friendship could be dearly bought, and
that letters could fall into mischievous hands
and be misconstrued. I congratulated myself that I knew one unselfish, cautious, dis-
cerning, far-seeing man, who would never
place a woman—if it rested with him—in a
compromising position.

And now! It is just great! And great
big Jack, the adviser, the oracle, sufficient
unto himself in all social, financial and worldly

matters, caught slipping! And he on the defensive with unsophisticated me! He says it all commenced a long time ago, when Under-the-Grass, Over-the-Grass — respectively—and he were bachelors together. And, to be sure, I would not now have known anything about it if I had not been with him when he opened the package, and the photograph and letter appeared to his gaze, to be welcomed with his big—awful big—" D."

Even then he would not have explained if I had not questioned seriously the honor and the manliness of his returning the photograph, with the letter, to her husband! Ye gods and little fishes! but it did seem a dreadful thing to do. Does yet. But Jack said the time had come when honor was on the other side. If I were a man I would say, as the millionaire once said about the public (seeing I am alone with no one to hear), " Honor be ——!"

But Jack said that he had given his word of honor to the husband, and back went that letter and the photograph. Then, Jack being on the defensive with me, told me the story.

.   .   .   .   .   .

Come to think it over, he did not tell me as much about the woman—himself and the

woman—as he did about the husband. He
said very little about the first days of his and
her acquaintance, when Cupid was firing the
arrows that resulted in these rapturous love-
letters. I suppose they were rapturous.
Men never do say much about that part of it
in after years. They only remember the cold
facts; the emotions, the illusions, the pulse
throbbing, the wear and tear on heart, brain
and nerves, get lost in the maze of other experiences which follow along afterward.

He did remember, however, that she was
fine looking, a fine dresser, a fine figure, a
dainty woman who was fond of him; who
told him, not at first, but after a while, of her
desolate and lonely life, and of how much he
had brightened it. And then she appealed
to him—his vanity probably. The vanity of
a man is marvelous if you strike it right.
She appealed to him until he used to write
her long letters, to make her life less desolate.
Jack told it all beautifully and tenderly.
Really, I myself felt quite sorry for the
woman. If it did not all seem to link together
evenly, naturally and humanly, it was due, of
course, to my own stupidity.

Then Jack said she became conscientious!

Women will get that way sometimes. It
strikes me strange that her conscience did not
go out a bit to Jack after she had gone so far
with him, but, woman-like, to assure Jack, I
suppose, of her being a good, naturally virtuous woman before he crossed her path, she
wrote him that she was going to tell her husband—the husband, too, who had caused the
desolation in her heart and left the loophole
for Jack.

Of course, Jack had to write more letters.
It must have made Jack forget his quiet dead-
elegance for a time. I will warrant his brow
knotted and his strong, direct, masterful way
went zigzag. I would like to have seen him
the day that the husband walked into his
office unannounced and turned the key in the
door. It must have been a tableau for a
drama! Then this man—a fine-looking fellow, Jack says—walking up to him and saying:

"Are you Mr. —— ?"

"I am," said Jack.

"Did you write these letters?" said the
man.

"I did," said Jack.

"You are a —— blackguard!" said the man.

"You are right," said Jack.

Then Jack gathered himself together. If husbands, in such cases, do not shoot immediately, they don't shoot at all, probably. Anyhow, Jack took a tumble to himself—being alone, I can use all the slang I want to—he arose to the situation, as it were. He said—and he must have said it sublimely:

"I am a blackguard to have written to your wife, and she is blameless. But I consider you a rascal. Any man that will allow his wife to travel about alone, from month to month, from year to year, and live days without speaking to her or making any attempts at reconciliation is a rascal, and deserves horsewhipping. If it were not for the publicity of the thing I would be tempted to chastise you myself. Your wife is a good woman, too good for you. Go back to her and ask her to forgive you."

And Jack won the day. The man—the husband—realized that he alone was the culprit. Jack's magnetism is wonderful. But he begged Jack to promise he would never write her another letter, and that he would

assist him to know and understand his wife
and help him to keep her; that no matter
what she did, he loved her, he would forgive
her, and would, in the future, live for her.

There was never a word from her since,
until the other day this photograph and letter
were sent back to the husband. Jack is surely
helping the husband to understand the wife.
Jack says that it is one couple well mated—
both idiots.

I am disappointed in Jack. Haven't analyzed it exactly, but——

IV.

Major remarked:

"Love seems to be playing a lot of pranks lately."

Lalla said in her sweet way:

"Is it really love—is it not mad infatuation, then the exposé, the censure and all that follows?"

Jack said nothing. He puffed away at his cigar and appeared to be waiting for me to say something. It is a way that he has lately. I am beginning to know Jack. I said nothing. I laughed. It was only a little laugh, but Jack threw away his cigar with such force that as it hit the railing of the piazza the fire, ashes and tobacco scattered all about. I really had to shake the skirt of my organdie. My laugh seemed to aggravate Jack. But surely it was better than to have said "I told you so"— that always sounds so—vulgar. W. Russell Ward's vanity had had a death-stab, and what

else was there for him to do but to commit
suicide ?

.   .   .   .   .   .

Reversing seems to be the motto of these
fin de siecle times. This man elopes with
Colonel Bradbury's wife. The authorities of
San Francisco—that portion which is banded
together to prevent vice—and the personally
interested friends of Mrs. Bradbury come to
the—her—rescue. She decides that she does
not love Mr. Ward—love, I suppose, would
skip through the iron bars of a jail even
sooner than through the window of poverty's
cottage. Prevention of vice and the friends
decide that she is too young or too beautiful,
or both, to be held responsible. She is released
from custody. Colonel Bradbury decides that
he has been neglectful and has not given his
own wife the attention that he should have
done, and he forgives her. He forgives her,
and takes her off on a pleasure trip to get ac-
quainted with her again.

.   .   .   .   .   .

This end of the century stands by the woman,
and the charming, fascinating man in the case
gets called baldheaded, plain, uninteresting,
penniless, and is abused generally. Society—

California society—discusses, debates and questions whether or no it must receive back again into its sacred fold Colonel and Mrs. Bradbury. Mr. and Mrs. Ward—Mrs. Ward has also come to the front with forgiveness and money for her husband—are left out of the discussion entirely. Society, however, worries itself into a wrinkle, two wrinkles between the eyes, trying to decide whether it is right or wrong to join hands with Colonel Bradbury and take back the runaway wife. The question is really a serious one. Mrs. Bradbury's escapade is so gilded with the husband's millions, and gold on the Pacific coast—well, Mrs. Bradbury's little "lark"—anyway, Mr. Ward's sin was bad, black, bold and penniless.

Sin and vice cannot afford to be poor if they hope to be forgiven. So the man in the case this time was deserted, then tabooed, then forgotten. His only capital was his personal fascinations, and when these failed him, and the end of the century showed him that the world was against him, and that he was to head the list, possibly, of what may be a new era, he could not bear it, and jumped to eternity from a flying train. It was not at all surprising.

. . . . . .

Jack, of course, had not agreed with me
when I said, some time ago, that Mr. Ward—
and men of his kind—could not endure the
stab to his vanity; that it was more than could
be expected of a man of the present day that
he should take up the lines of life again without a loophole for him to tell anything but
the exact truth and face facts and his wife;
that he had not the moral courage to stand
truthfully by the episode to the mother of his
children, and to go on year after year with
the knowledge that he could never again have
her trust and confidence. It was not the
wrong thing that would worry him so much
but that he must confess to actual guilt, and
would have no explanation through which he
could again build up her faith.

.   .   .   .   .   .

Men do not consider their unworthiness,
but they do struggle and fight against losing
this blind faith of a wife. Something pecu-
liar about it. That faith—the faith of an un-
worldly-wise woman—seems to be, to them,
their one chance, one hope of forgiveness and
heaven at the end. They juggle with it, they
trifle with it, they strain it to the very verge
of the precipice. They, themselves, will

sometimes slip over the edge and cling with
bleeding finger-tips to the jagged, projecting
rocks, then clamber back again, hold out the
bleeding fingers for the wife to dress the
wounds, and while her own heart is breaking
with what natural common sense tells her
must be his faithlessness, he will say: " Dearie,
have you still faith in me ?"

Instinctively she knows this faith of hers is
her one chance of happiness; her one hold ; her
hand that is holding something sure for him
at the last, when he will be through with all
that is searing her heart now, and making her
wonder if her tears are the reward for the
truth and loyalty she is giving to him.

So she says: " Yes, I have faith in you."

He gives a sigh of relief, which she takes
for one of happiness, and he forthwith pats
himself on the back metaphorically, smooths
out his conscience philosophically, and has
faith again in himself and his innocence.

But when a positive knowledge must stand
in the way of this faith, this one hope, then
the fingers must unclasp from the projecting
rocks and he falls down to death—first, the
social one, then the eternal one—what else ?

    .   .   .   .   .   .

But, of course, Jack had not agreed with me, though I did express all these opinions of mine very mildly. There's a "rift in the lute" of Jack's and my friendship, anyway. We are still "good fellows," but as a real good fellow I do not feel that Jack did right in telling me about the woman to whom he gave his sympathy and wrote the letters. It is a mistake for men to be too frank with women. Frankness, to be sure, is an admirable quality, but truths are brutal at best. They strike somewhere. It is all very well for a man to say: "I want you to know the truth, and not think it is worse than it is, or that I am better than I am," but when he goes into detail to establish your confidence in him, he tells you of his own affair, certainly, but he also tells you the affair of the other one. It is not all his own secret. He betrays her confidence, though he may not tell you her name, and you wonder how soon he will be discussing you in this cold-blooded, deliberate manner to convince some new attraction that he is a man to be trusted, because he is perfectly "frank."

. . . . . .

If men will have affairs, the least they can do is to hold them inviolate, and not try to

win the confidence of one by betraying the
trust of another.   No man, husband, brother
or friend is ever called upon or should get
caught in a trap that will make him lisp a
word of his affairs with women.   Silence is
what wins confidence that is worth having,
and the man who can keep silent under pres-
sure—well, I believe I could give him even
my own confidence.

It sounds fine, grand to hear your bachelor
friend say to you that he would never marry
without making "a clean breast of it," then
commence life anew.   But I wonder if it
should happen that the women whom he has
known should also make a clean breast of it
whether he would commence life anew this
side or the other side of the "dark river."

.   .   .   .   .   .

When I saw that my little laugh so aggra-
vated Jack that he could throw away that fine
cigar, of course, I did not wait for him to get
started into his vehement assertions that admit of no argument—from women.   I said,
reflectively:

"It seems sad that this man Ward could not
have said to his wife before he died that he
was sorry, and taken away, in a measure, the

memory that another woman had heard his last words of love. It will always stand between her and even her mother-love for his children."

The Major and Lalla agreed with me. Jack still said nothing, but lit another cigar.

V.

The old Colonel sends me this letter, and asks me what I think of it.   Poor old Colonel ! How helpless he is !   In his old age he hunts for romance, and finds that every minute of his charmer's time—the time given to him—is worth just so much of gold.   He says he loves her as a daughter, and she cuts him " to the heart in her ingratitude."

How she hates him, and how she does love his millions !   This letter, to one who thoroughly knows the woman, is most amusing.   I must read it again :

                 " —— —— STREET, PHILADELPHIA.

" My DEAR COLONEL : I am writing to-night, and somehow I think it is the last letter I shall ever write.   At this time, with the drama all played out, and at the *finale*—which means the curtain-call of life—I want to say that I have always appreciated your great kindness to me, and, at the same time, I want to comment on the phrase you used to my sweet and dear friend, Mrs. M—— ' the good die young.'" [*That* is an awful slip of intelligence. I wonder just what she means? The good die young! I can see those two women as she wrote that. It is ambiguously expressed, but it was meant to make a hit with the audience—the Colonel.] "I leave it all without regret, save that you should think, after all you have done for me, I should be unworthy it all. I have never been that—but let it rest in its grave—your grievances and my own. I am too weak to write more, too ill to write intelligently; but at the last, dear, we lie down to die and forget.

"Good-night.

"M——."

"I should so love to see you!"

So the Colonel has been refusing to see her or to give her any more money. Dying—this time.

.   .   .   .   .   .

There's a little straggling of the handwriting toward the end—properly weak from exhaustion, where "we lie down to die and forget," but she seems to have gathered her forces again where she "would so love" to see him —that line is as firm as the first one. This last letter of a dying woman is written with

pen and ink, carefully punctuated, and with
the letters all gracefully flourished as a finish
to the words. The Colonel says in his letter
that M—— has never written a letter so kind,
and what do I think of it; and do I think she
can be really ill? Poor Colonel! After all
the trouble he has had, the estrangement from
his family, his own belief in her duplicity, he
cannot yet understand to what depths women
of this kind can go in their greed for luxuries.
What do I think of it—the letter, the woman,
and the game? I think she would order a
casket and a funeral cortege to accomplish her
purpose.

.   .   .   .   .   .

"Dearie, you are so gullible about women,"
was a favorite expression of Over-the-Grass.
I never disputed the assertion. I really
thought him a better judge of feminine proclivities than I was myself. I discovered mistakes often in my estimates of women, and
would drop the acquaintances. He made no
mistakes, neither did he know them no more;
he clung—clung once too often. I'm sure I
was not gullible about Miss C——. From the
first I was perplexed and annoyed. Then a
sort of grim humor and a resignation to the

inevitable took the place of doubt and perplex-
ity. I was perplexed in the explanations of
Miss C——'s environments—her explanations ;
what she called " distinctively honest, though it
might be bohemian," was not at all clear to
me. I was annoyed that she should so cling
to me, a stranger—herself in the midst of people, with whose names, history and present
life she seemed familiar—among them and
not of them. She would cling to me, tower-
ing above me, on the beach, in the water, on
the piazza of the hotel, and I found myself
seated at her table the first time I went into
the dining-room after meeting her—an in-
struction she had given to the waiter without
consulting me. The grim humor, and the
amusement at the inevitable, came in my
fruitless endeavor to drop her without being
unkind, and in my awakening to the fact that
I might be figuring as one of a pair in this
Summer hotel where, surely, Miss C—— was
not a social favorite—even where the social
leaders were the wives of clerks and salesmen
of democratic John Wanamaker. It was
amusing and worth the flip of a penny to see
which would interest me the most—society as
I found it, or this " distinctively honest bo-

hemian"—until my friends should arrive. The
penny coming down in favor of the "bohemian," I proceeded to study her as a type of
the class we hear about, but seldom have the
opportunity to know.

. . . . . .

She was like the "Ancient Mariner"—needing some one to whom she could tell her story.
She needed an audience who could realize the
fine points of her play. She liked me, unless
at times I inadvertently showed I was not
believing in the truth of the plot, and was
unwise enough to express myself—then I was
"very rude." I was rude. She was not a
woman to me. I must have felt as men do
sometimes toward women whom they do not
respect. The only way to make her feel was
to tell her the truth, devoid of all flattery.
She existed on the old Colonel's money; she
thrived on flattery and admiration. But what
a time she did have getting the money!
Scrubbing floors in a Spanish prison would
have been easier.

. . . . . .

She introduced herself to me in the water,
and said she had met me the summer before.
I knew she hadn't, but I was alone, and I had

noticed her at the hotel, so let her talk. From
the first she seemed bursting with items about
herself. She always labeled everything with
her great "mentality," her intellectual acquire-
ments, her great but suppressed talent as an
actress. Her beauty, fine figure and power
over men came next. She chatted constantly
about her writings, her ambitions, her poems
and prose, her friends—but her guardian in-
terfered with her friends. He, the guardian,
was an old man, jealous, had her money in-
vested, and would not allow her to look at a
man. If she did look at men she received no
money. She said she was twenty-four, and
he, the guardian, she thought, was seventy-
four. He said he was fifty-four, but he was
toothless and tottering. Somehow these Philadelphia women never get beyond twenty-
four in the years. She looked buxom, beefy
and mature. In any place but Philadelphia I
am sure one would think she had made a mistake in the years.

.   .   .   .

She had a cottage up in the mountains.
She made the Colonel think she was ill and
would go into retirement while he was in
Europe—she would miss him so. He gave

her a thousand dollars and sailed away. She
bought this little tumble-down cottage way off
by itself in a picturesque spot—it was a picture, as she described it—and there she rested.
Up there was a professor of the State Uni-
versity, who also had a cottage near by and
away from the worry of the world. To this
cottage came other professors and prominent
authors. There were intellectual feasts and
stories, and poems written in collaboration.
And there was love-making. The professor
taught her to love. The professor was an
artist at love-making. When she would quote
these well-known names so familiarly, a look
of doubt or some question I would ask, would'
make her read me his letters, to convince me
that she was telling the truth. Once the professor was ill; she went to the hospital to read
to him. His wife came in one day and found
her there. This was before the cottage was
bought. There came near being a divorce—
papers were drawn up. The wife was finally
persuaded to think better of it. There must
be no scandal in a professor's life; but the
wife was a drag. Then came the cottage and
the quiet for the professor. Then the cottage,
with its romance, love and life itself—for

Miss C——came to grief. She wrote her most passionate letter, and sent some fruit and flowers to the professor when she returned to the city. His wife had arrived in the meantime at the home on the hillside. She—the wife—mistook the " Mr." for " Mrs." opened the letter, returned it, also the fruit and flowers. Now she was writing to the professor in care of a friend.

.   .   .   .   .   .

The professor's letters were life to her, but so were also the letters of Frank C.—Frank had loved her for years. He also had a putty-faced wife, who did not appreciate him. His letters did not have the intellectual flow of the professor, but they would grace quite well the pages of a love story. Then the gentleman in Baltimore, to whom she was engaged, she would probably marry. Here was Ned N——'s; he had loved her two years; he had told her yesterday how beautiful she was, and that he was trying, for his daughter's sake, to stop his promiscuous flying around, and was also trying to set an example for his wife, who always followed the pace he led. His wife she hated. His wife had asked some-one if Miss C——was " still posing for a bohe-

mian saint." She would tell it all to me, with
a voice which showed conclusively that she
had studied elocution, but in a way, with such
a mixture of romance and truth, that I could
only think of the lines:

> And even love, by difference nice,
> Becomes a virtue or a vice,

and give her the benfit of some doubts. She
was fascinating until you tired of her. Her
figure was rather attractive in evening dress,
but disappointing in short bathing costume.
When she was not telling the story of her
loves, her father, her stepmother, she filled in
about the old Colonel, and had long ago to me
given up the name of "guardian." When
her father cast her adrift she met him accidentally. She was ill from trying to earn a
living. She had failed as an actress, and now
was simply making a stage of her life. She
appealed to his sympathies and chivalry,
worked on his weakest points and prejudices,
pretended to be ill, pretended to love him,
and finally succeeded in getting his support.
She hated him so there were times that she
felt that she could kill him. She really hated
him, but she discovered that the more she
hated him the more he loved her "hellish-

ness." And that was the way she managed
him.

.   .   .   .   .   .

Then I met the Colonel. He told me she
was as dear to him as a daughter could be.
He loved her purely and unselfishly. The
next day he hated her, did not respect her;
she deceived him; and he had, with his own
eyes, seen her talking to a man on the piazza
of the hotel. Never another cent of his
money should she have. He seemed to mean
it. Just then she needed money badly. She
talked baby talk to him, went driving with
him, to luncheons, dinners, and was agreeable. Then she—in the room adjoining mine
—remained in bed four days, too ill to see anyone but a handsome young physician. At the
end of that time came the check she wanted.
And I hear, since then, she has been very much
of an invalid most of the time, getting well
only when money or check arrives.

What is this?

Another letter from the Colonel. Miss
C—— is better, and has sent word that she
will meet him at the —— hotel to dine with
him. He must have been particularly generous with her this time.

VI.

Jack and I are evidently "out" for the present. He is remaining away until he gets my answer. If Jack were his old self, a little thing such as asking a woman to marry him, and getting no answer, would not keep him away. But Jack is so changed lately. I felt all that honesty of his meant something. When his kind becomes conscientious, honest, direct and open with you about themselves and their private affairs one may as well decide it means something serious. It is serious enough now —Jack actually asking me to marry him! He should have more sense. I could shake, literally shake him—spoiling everything! He should know, or he ought to know, my opinions. Anyhow, what, with Under-the-Grass and Over-the-Grass, would I do with Jack? It must take some courage, however, for a man to want to marry a woman with two "pasts." Probably he consoled himself thinking there was surely nothing hidden in my life. To a bachelor with some "pasts" of his own this may be a consolation, but to me

that is the worst of it ; everybody knows as
well as Jack—that is not the worst just now.
The worst is Jack himself.

.   .   .   .   .   .

Why *did* he?—wrote it, too! He tried to
talk it, and blundered like a schoolboy, giving
me the opportunity to misunderstand and to
turn the conversation into another channel.
I scarcely knew Jack ; it was so entirely different from his usual cool, careless, command-
ing self. It almost rattled me. Then finally
for him to take a mean advantage and write
it? Fifteen pages of me on a pedestal, and
debonair, nonchalant bachelor Jack ready to
devote the rest of his life to keeping me there!
I never thought it of Jack. Of course, I did
not write much in answer; as Reta says, "Am
not built that way." Letters are bad things—
such conclusive evidence to have held in the
background. We are "out" really because I
did not go into detail on paper. Jack said he
could not believe that I would be so cold and
vague—or was I calculatingly cautious?—in a
matter of this kind, where with him heart,
soul and life itself were at stake. Had I no
real feeling ?

.   .   .   .   .   .

That was it. It was real feeling in me. I
am too fond of Jack to say no, and too fond
of—of myself to say yes. One could say
" no " verbally in a careless way and leave a
doubt, and have a friend. To write " no "
would settle it, unless you smoothed things
over with reason. And how would my reasons look on paper? How would it look in
black and white for me to say that these six
or eight months of freedom have—are beginning to have a spice of joy in them—joy,
actual, alive joy after all I have suffered ? I
pinch myself to see if this be I. I could talk
things to Jack if necessary, but I do not want
to go on record as saying that the " spice "
comes not so much in the release from matri-
monial bonds as from the conventional ones.

    .   .   .   .   .   .

It makes little difference whether you are
in the right or not, when the court comes to
your rescue women are not your friends.
Every woman in your old set seems to consider you as wanting her husband or her sweetheart. At first you wonder at it. Then,
remembering their great devotion to you when
you were the wife of a handsome man, you
decide they must have secretly looked upon

you as somewhat of a rival in those days in the attentions of your husband, and are now gauging you and the danger to their own husbands by their own bygone proclivities. You decide to join the ranks of what some term "Upper Bohemia."

In this atmosphere you begin to realize the delights of living. There are sorrows to be forgotten, but there is a contented present and some solid hopes of a peaceful future.

.   .   .   .   .   .

It is being "on earth again." A woman with a "past"—or even two of them—and with an untrammelled present, is more or less interesting to men. She is a mystery. The mystery is that they cannot quite believe that a woman with knowledge, cut loose from all fetters, is proof against all temptation. She "queens it" while they study her. Interest in a woman is only a step from love for her, and—dear me! I was forgetting all about Jack.

.   .   .   .   .   .

What am I going to do with Jack—he bothers me so! All at once, too, after all these years of that lovely diamond-cut-diamond friendship of ours—no outwardly expressed

sentiment. Sometimes I have caught glances
and gleams from Jack's eyes, but whatever
real sentiment there is in a man like Jack he
holds in check until his time comes—though
it may not be for years. Across rooms and in
crowds I have seen that look in the dark eyes,
and at times in our gay life—the pace struck
by Over-the-Grass—I felt a security in having
Jack near. Without any attentions that
might cause comment, or even notice, he
always seemed to have provided for my protection and comfort and well-being—if Over-
the-Grass was too busy. There were occasional books and flowers; but that was all. It
all appeared to be unconscious on his part, or
mere habit. Personally, we seemed to be
continually sharpening our steels. But lately
all that has changed. Jack has not been Jack.
His big, brawny independence and assertive
manner have deserted him. He is kind and attentive, but says it breaks him all up to see me
getting sceptical and losing all that old trust
and faith that was a part of my nature; that
it jars upon him to see me so gay—and then
he changed the word "gay" to happy.
When I challenged the thing, and asked him
if I should mourn forever for—for the insult

I had received, there was a pleading look in his eyes, but he was silent. But the other night, when I fell from my wheel, as that equestrian nearly rode me down, and Jack picked me up, with that—that tenderness, I knew it was—knew what it all meant—but did not think he would ever tell me of it.

.   .   .   .   .   .

And contrary, woman-like—like me—I haven't been nearly so interested in him since. Now, if, in his old way—before he became frank, honest and open about himself, and before I discovered this—this new thing, he had strode in with his hands in his pockets and, in matter-of-fact tone, had said: "See here, little girl, I am going to marry you. How long will it take you to get your togs in shape?" I really believe I would have said meekly—well, it would not surprise me if I had gotten ready. But to let me discover my power over him! It is the wrong thing with a woman like myself. I will not marry Jack for a good many reasons, but principally because he is so easily managed.

.   .   .   .   .   .

Come to think of it, it is very strange, under any circumstances, that he should stay away

three days. The strangeness of it is probably
cause for my giving him all these thoughts
for the last hour or so. . . . There's the
bell. Jack and Reta! . . . Well!!!
Such cool audacity! Jack is evidently himself again! One would not suppose this man
had written a letter with all that "feeling
heart and soul," and the rest of it. I am truly
glad that my answer was vague and cold, and
his question still unanswered. I am glad that
no opportunity has presented itself to talk the
matter over verbally. I might have really
shown emotion myself, and said—almost anything. But now! It will be a long time now
before there will be an answer. To think of
his turning back as if with an afterthought as
he and Reta were going out and saying : " By
the way, never mind that little difference of
ours; it will keep. No hurry."

Has he changed his mind or is he trying to
manage me ?

VII.

Jack is really quite a comfort again. If it
were not for this long "offguard" letter of
his, I should think, at times, that I had dreamed
that he had asked me to marry him. Anyhow,
it is much more convenient and soothing for
me to forget, and to forget also that he has
not, as yet, had an answer. His cool afterthought, "no hurry," even if it hit my vanity,
helped me out of the quandary I surely was
in ; I would not say yes, I could not say no.

. . . . . .

I wonder why I could not answer. Analyzed closely, it is probably all due to that inevitable human trait, perversity. And it is
my opinion that perversity is a species of insanity, and that we are all lunatics.

. . . . . .

Now, here's Jack; and here is myself—
friends for years. Jack is a man of honor,
and would not love, or "make love" to, the
wife of his friend. Over-the-Grass himself
was always loyal to men, even if honor could

slip with—but I must not think of Over-the-
Grass.   Bachelor Jack was, perhaps—with
all due respect to his nicety of honor—all the
more interested because of the insurmount-
able barriers.

.   .   .   .   .   .

For myself, Jack was interesting, because—
well, a sphinx couldn't surpass him.   Then,
when opportunity came—the friend caught in
a social trap, which forced the snapping of
legal chains—the sphinx was, after all, only a
man, with a man's great loving heart; mine
if I would have it.   Then this little imp, perversity, comes trotting in; what was the use
of committing myself just now?   An answer
would destroy all romance and make affairs so
commonplace.   Words spoken or written—
dear me!   After you have lived a bit in this
swirling, swishing life of ours—what are
words? Nothing.   How *much* a glance!—
the half frown on the forehead, the slight
raising of the eyebrow; the direct look of a
man, the half-drooping eyelids of a woman—
the one revealing, the other concealing the
soul.   A glance kindles the fire in the heart,
words satisfy, or dissatisfy the cold reasoning
of the brain.   One is an exquisite dream, the

other a practical fact.   And as Adelaide says,
" Dreams never pall."

.   .   .   .   .   .

But when the dreaming is over and the fact
must be faced there comes this little human
devil—perversity. We want that which we
cannot have, and we care not for what we can
have. We do not go beyond the present during the insane attack and weigh the happiness
of the days and years to come ; we simply allow this little devil to dance its jig, though
we know it may leave and is making the worst
kind of a heartache.

.   .   .   .   .   .

Troubles are divided into two classes—one
controlled by a big-horned, cloven-footed devil,
and the other by the snippy little devil which
flashes in and out of our hearts. The big
devil is usually placed in our paths by others.
It follows us. Sometimes we can evade it,
and then again it catches us up on its horns
and gives us a toss. We come down into the
dust, with all courage, ambition and hope absorbed in despair. We can pick ourselves up
and be desperate, with all that is best in us so
deadened that even our consciences cannot
hear a whisper ; or we can, in there action, be

taken completely out of our own selfishness
and be lifted to a moral and mental victory
and to all that is noblest in ourselves and humanity.

.   .   .   .   .   .

But this little devil—this imp—this insane
perversity of human nature gets its hold on us
whether we will or not.   It makes us for the
time ignore all that is best in ourselves and in
others—it is a part of us.   We recognize its
clutch and try to get away from it.   A colossal trouble brought in on the horns of the big
devil we can rise above, and feel sometimes
that our minds and hearts have been broadened in the ride; but this little devil, though
we know well it is all within ourselves, will
cause our tears to flow and our sorrows to pile
up.   It is all a fictitious substance, with possibly a mint of happiness lying below.   We
are conscious of it all, but this insanity makes
us ignore it sometimes for so long that the little imp gets in its work and the opportunity
is lost.

.   .   .   .   .   .

I must simply call a halt on this moralizing.
What is the matter with me ?   Surely I am
not perverse; I am sensible.   It is the calcu-

lating sense that comes with the hard knocks of experience. And then, too, Jack's getting no answer seems of little importance to him. Still I notice that no one else gets on the track—his track—my track. He is again carelessly indifferent in his manner, but he is not neglecting me. It was amusing when these flowers arrived. There being no card attached I was not supposed to know from whom they came. Jack said:

"Where is the card? What, no card? Someone must consider himself on sure footing to send such a quantity of magnificent flowers without a card."

"They might have been sent by someone who only wished to give me pleasure, with no thought of himself," I said quietly.

"Y-e-s," he said, slowly, "if it had been me I would have undoubtedly spread myself all over the card, or a lot of paper with some nonsense I did not mean," and then he added, carelessly, "*adios mia cara*," and went away.

I might worry a little about my own perverseness and about Jack, but it is time to worry when a man, a man like Jack, is not attentive.

VIII.

"Pasts" are not so bad if it were not for
some of the memories that cling to them.
Memories that cling to others, or the knowledge of a "past" makes you of interest, attractive to men, a menace to the imagination
of women, but the memories that hover about
yourself are sometimes like truths—brutal.
Memory is the scar of truth's cruel wound.

.   .   .   .   .   .

Somehow, to-night I cannot get away from
memory. It seems as if an avalanche of these
cruel truths confronted my mental vision. At
every instance these truths struck a blow that
left a scar as deep and unsightly as any made
by the knife. There were tragedies in every
one. The first one that comes to me was the
one I struck my self when I said to Under-
the-Grass—it seems sacrilegious to-night to
apply that name to him—"My love is dead."

.   .   .   .   .   .

Ah, me, but I was young then!—a child in
years, a novice in experience. The world

was good, or it was bad. There were, in
those days in my 'teens, no happy mediums,
no philosophies, through which the peccadilloes of men and women could be excused,
gauged and forgiven.   And I had walked the
floor through the long hours of the night,
waiting and watching—for what? Only for
a husband to come home! I smile now. And
it is perfectly true that my trusting love had
died in those hours of suspense.   It was the
first experience. In after years we do not
build our loves on such frail foundations.
But when love is young, very young, and the
world is new everything is rose-colored, or
deep black night.

.   .   .   .   .   .

It is true that my trusting love had died in
those hours of suspense—not at first. At first,
when the hours of waiting commenced, I saw
him a mangled corpse, the victim of some
horrible accident—anything and *everything*
that was awful! It must be awful to make
him forget that I would be anxious and would
suffer. Again I smile. Men do spoil women.
When my faithful emissary, who could not
endure that I should suffer so, returned with
the report   that   Under-the-Grass—really

that name does not sound so sacrilegious as I
recall the circumstance—that Under-the-
Grass had ridden away in a carriage with
some jolly and singing companions, my heart
in its relief took on a sensation it had never
before felt. Love was dead. It could mean
nothing else. And so I told him.

.   .   .   .   .   .

My blow struck. A deathly white came
into his face and a look into his eyes that I
had never seen before. It was as if his hope
for heaven had gone. It was first love with
him and me. It was the first lesson in life to
me. To him it was the first glimpse of the
coldness that can come into a loving heart, the
first knowledge that a girl's heart, though
elastic, can stand only just so much. It was
trust gone, and the first reef taken in the sails
of love's boat. I knew so little then. Now—
well, now—I would not walk now. I would
calmly retire. I would know that these little
trifles are not due so much to cruel thought-
lessness, and the fact that you are forgotten,
as to a champagnely-erratic head. You learn
a lot after the first lesson.

.   .   .   .   .   .

But I have never forgotten the look that
came into the beautiful boyish eyes—we were

but boy and girl—nor the quiver to the lips
when he faltered, "don't say that." Now
that the years have gone by and these truths
array themselves before me I seem to see and
feel that blow that I struck as though I had
been the sufferer. It was then the awakening to the hard realities of life and to the
anguish the heart is capable of holding.
Though the sweetest part of love, the absolute
trust, died then, and the heart lost its light-
ness, never again to return—in those years
the heart is so light it seems almost impossible to keep it in its place—it all comes back
vividly. Out of it and all that has come and
gone since then, the tenderest memory with
me to-night is that pleading look in those dark
eyes that are now closed forever.

.   .   .   .   .   .

Then came the blow struck by Over-the-
Grass. It was what the boys call a stag-
gerer." I am smiling again. Gracious! do
I know myself? It is an actual fact that I
am smiling now at my terrible suffering then.
He said :

" What if I should tell you that I love that
woman with my heart and soul ?"

.   .   .   .   .   .

I heard the words, but my brain must have

been dull. "That" woman was so dreadfully low. She was one of the vampires that exist, God knows better than I for what reason. And she was the woman that all the world came to know about; a woman so morbid and so vulgar that her name could not be mentioned without the air being defiled. I had heard, and as the meaning finally waded through my dulled senses, I said:

"You, *you* love a woman like *that?*"

.   .   .   .   .   .

And then all there was in life, in heaven, in eternity, seemed to float away and a horrible black cloud wrapped itself around me and suffocated me. As it partially cleared away I could hear his voice saying:

"My baby, my darling, I lied to you—I lied to you. It is you I love—only you. God pity me! You are my life—she is my curse."

But it was the truth. He must have loved her. With me it had been the love of my womanhood; the love that comes with experience and that overlooks, forgives and loves again, that gives friendship, truth and loyalty.

.   .   .   .   .   .

For days I was dazed. Then the end came. It was an accident—an hour for a last good-

bye.   But the good-bye chanced to be to me,
and not to her.   The hour was fatal, because
before it was over everybody and—this time
—myself knew he was with her.   The final
crash came with its crushing sorrows and brain
tortures, but the blow that left the deepest
wound was the one struck with those few
words of truth.

.   .   .   .   .   .

I am here myself, and my friends say I do
not show any great grief.   I wonder to myself, however, if ever again I will feel any up-
lifting joy or any heartrending sorrow?   I
presume I will, being that I am still a woman.

IX.

And so Over-the-Grass says I ruined his life. *I*—good Heaven!

.   .   .   .   .   .

I am really knocked out. There are just now no philosophies in my vocabulary with which to meet this. With Over-the-Grass out of my life I have learned to smile and to be amused at the jig fate has danced with me. I seemed in every way such a featherweight. But to run up against him accidentally—my smile froze. I have no philosophies, and I am so tired that, as I sink into these pillows, I feel that I have no physical strength.

.   .   .   .   .   .

I had learned to bear patiently—patience! I hate the word! . . . I know that I must be knocked out. Otherwise I would not be hating anything any more than I am loving anything—those all-disturbing days are over. But patience? No. I took the inevitable as any one should take it—just took it. I have come to the time in these few months that I can smile at myself—myself as I was

then. I can smile, have been smiling for
some time, that less than a year ago the earth
seemed slipping—did slip from under my
feet. It slipped away and left me in space
where I had to grope blindly for a foothold
on which to stand to grasp life again. When
I found it, idols, dreams, certainties, ambitions
and hopes were piled up in such a confused
wreck that out of the débris nothing could be
saved with which to make a foundation for
drifting through the future. There was nothing left of the old life but myself. All bridges
into the past—outside of memory's walls—had
to be burned. I burned them—the court
and I.

    .   .   .   .   .   .

It was all, from every side, a terrible thing!
to stand before the world a wife, yet not a
wife—or a widow, yet not a widow. Of the
two a " widow, yet not a widow," was preferable. I could do nothing else.

    .   .   .   .   .   .

It was the last act of the drama in the life
of Over-the-Grass and myself. So many
acts had been played. There had to be a final
one. The ending of the others had been as
he would have—forgiveness. Men have in

them such depths for penitence and remorse. It is equaled only by their capacity for pleasure. If one should not forgive and give them a chance at things again, one would feel herself the wrong-doer. So you forgive, but you realize there is a great affinity between penitence and satiety. If remorse would only forewarn; but one cannot make over the world.

. . . . . .

I finally burned the bridges into the past, but it was after I had tried, with all my soul, to save something from the wreck that I saw floating toward me. Intuitively I stepped aboard the wreck—the boat that was even then sinking. I felt it going down, with every moral support gone, and, without knowing the facts, plead with him—and—my God! I stifle and my face burns as I recall it—I plead with her.

. . . . . .

I would not have discovered so much intuitively if she had not appropriated him before me—not knowing that I was his wife. Involuntarily—after the shock of realizing—I asked him which it was, that woman or me. I asked the question. It must have been for effect.

Perhaps I wanted her to know. Of course I
knew. It could only be me. . . . My
smile is not altogether frozen, knockout or
not. It was her—in the end. At that time,
under those circumstances, it was a hard question for him to answer. Before him stood his
wife, whom he could not give up, and there
also was the woman, whom he—could not
give up.

.   .   .   .   .   .

Life, as I knew it, really seemed very dear
to me then. I must have appeared quite dra-
matic. I actually plead for what was my own.
I felt so much, yet knew so little. Somehow,
the future and life itself were certainly tottering. So I plead with him and with her. Not
for myself—his father's gray hairs seemed of
more importance just then. For myself, I
was too hurt, too bruised, too—there was,
however, one thing—there must be no scene,
no scandal : that first, hearts could come afterward.

The minutes ticked by into hours, and each
minute seared itself into my brain.

.   .   .   .   .   .

I have learned to smile since. She did the
smiling that day. Once she laughed aloud.

It must have been very ridiculous to her. I
was, really, toward the end, pleading that the
respected name of a man remain untarnished.
She, years before, had lost trace of the value
of a good and respected name. She gauged
life in its importance through notoriety. I
could have gone on my knees, even to a woman
of her kind, to avoid it. She smiled and
would not go out of his life.

. . . . . .

Ah, well, I plead for much that seemed
very dear to me that day. I think there were
times that I could have forgiven and have
been made to believe that I was not generous
in my understanding of the situation, and that
possibly I was unreasonable, even plebeian
enough to be jealous—jealous! Now I *am*
smiling. I am really myself again. I will
get up from this couch and take a good whiff
at these lovely flowers—I wonder if there is a
card this time? Yes—dear Jack!

. . . . . .

Yes, I plead with the woman and with
Over-the-Grass and did all I could to avert the
crash, but it came. And to-day I met him.
He said that I was hasty—the court and I—
in burning those bridges—that I knew that he

was not himself; that he could not have gone away with her if he had been in his right senses; that I had ruined his life; that I should have forgiven him once more!

This must be the reward a woman receives for forgiving at all.

X.

Popular men, like popular actors, make bad husbands—they cannot endure the inanity, the tameness of an audience of one.

.   .   .   .   .   .

Something there is that is overpowering in the luxury of my den to-night. It is the sachets, the scented pillows—Jettine must have freshened them to-day; the lamplight, mellowed into a half glow by the tinted shade; dull grayish blue in the silken walls, the cool, restful color that seems a fitting background for this couch, pillows and canopied drapery, with its dark Egyptian red and suppressed yellows, greens, olives and antique blues, brought in the mingling to a quiet tone that suggests bursting any minute into a mad, passionate rioting.

.   .   .   .   .   .

My pretty den! Just this couch, with its apparently innumerable pillows piled onto it, around it and tumbled from it to the different parts of the room; a pure, dainty, translucent marble Phryne, with bowed head and face

buried against tapering arm, and delicate back,
curved into lines that until now had known
only love, outlined against the dull blue; a
white fur rug ; a slow-burning gas grate, with
its moss-covered log, with the moss igniting,
burning red, curling, disappearing and light-
ing again ; an inviting easy-chair, a "sleepy
hollow" near; an escritoire ; the scent of the
roses, or the violet, or whatever it is that
makes it so unusually luxuriant to-night.   It is
luxuriant luxury, sacred to myself and these
" Reveries."

.   .   .   .   .   .

I close my eyes and float away into ether.
This ether—this space—seems to hold my
astral body, and I look down and around and
over this pink-and- white thing—myself.   In
looking down with clear astral eyes, I wonder
if that little, insignificant blonde bundle lying
in among the pillows, with one slippered foot
hanging over the edge of the couch, herself
all decked out in lace frills and furbelows,
can have—with that baby face—lived and
loved, and have been the cause of some finished
and more unfinished tragedies!

.   .   .   .   .   .

Tragedy? Yes, that is what it is—this bo-

ing or having been the wife of a popular man.
It is one long-continued play, with its thrill-
ing parts enacted behind the scenes. When a
man is popular—very, very popular—like the
leading man of a successful theatrical company
—he cannot thrive contentedly without the
applause of the many. His life becomes a con-
tinued string of posing. In private life a reaction sets in. He must have diversion or
stagnate. The play goes on. Sometimes he
allows his brute nature to get on the rampage
without check. Sometimes the flattery he has
received outside is mixed with sparkling bev-
erages, and behind the scenes, with no one—
but one—to see or understand, sensational
tragedies are worked up with the *finale* in the
middle and with no logical curtain.

.   .   .   .   .   .

It was really very funny—afterward—when
Over-the-Grass actually went so far as to
make his will. At first during these playful
periods I was really as good as a packed house.
No actor could have wished for more effect.
I did not know for such a long time that it
was acting. It was real to me—of course the
real effect of champagne, or absinthe, or something—I did not know just what, but *some-*

thing—but how could I decide what the result would be?

.   .   .   .   .   .

Oh, yes, I was a capital audience. While there was no danger of my calling assistance —in my horror of outsiders witnessing these scenes—I myself run the whole gamut of emotions. This night, somehow—I must have been dull or else the play was getting old—I sat by while Over-the-Grass prepared to commit suicide. He was on a mad hunt for happiness. And once before I had almost died in my fright; I staggered and fell, but did not die— neither did Over-the-Grass. He said it was all due to a cocktail or two that he had mixed or drank before the champagne. Consequently this night I was apparently unmoved. He prepared a deadly dose. I calmly looked on and waited for him to take it.

.   .   .   .   .   .

I was sorry then, and have been sorry ever since when thinking about it, that I did not know how to smoke a cigarette. It would have accentuated my coolness in such a lovely way if I could have asked Over-the-Grass just then for a light. My heart was quaking—not knowing how far he would go to break up my

calm—but I sat back among the pillows—
thank Heaven, not these pillows—with my
hands back of my head and the laces falling
away from my arms—posing a bit myself—
looking at him and waiting. He was in this
scene he was acting not supposed, of course,
to notice little details. It was death—'sdeath
—he was courting—death he would have in a
minute—only one minute more.

.   .   .   .   .   .

I still waited. It was strychnia in a hypo-
dermic syringe. He gave a side glance. I
settled a little more comfortably. I would
have yawned, but it would have been so inex-
pressibly rude, even with one's own husband,
at such a time. He laid the little instrument
down and said, "My God! I have not made
my will—what would have become of you, my
baby, my darling?"

I didn't know. He made his will—without
witnesses. I have it yet. It took some time.
The little instrument disappeared among the
papers, though he forgot about his hunt for
happiness in the argument with himself
whether it would be loyal or right for me to
marry again. Then came melancholy, then
sleep, then penitence and remorse.

.   .   .   .   .   .

My astral body does not stay in space as I recall the touch of cold steel which I have felt many a time on my temple and against my heart. I tumble back into myself and start upright at the luxury and safety of my den. Cold steel is cold, and such a little accident might send the bullet ploughing its way to your death.

.   .   .   .   .   .

But it is all a part of the play. Just the sensational reaction of the actor or of the popular man—the very popular man—in private life; the popular man under the influence of outside flattery and a few social drinks.

XI.

It is strange that Jack should so dislike that word " bohemia." One would suppose that he, naturally, would be the one to revel in it. To me—as I have analyzed the term—he was the difference, the fine line, between the bohemian and the vagabond. I had gotten so that I really had an affection for the term.

But Jack says no; that I must not use the word; that use it as I will, in its highest sense, it smacks of the half world, the no world, of sawdust, beer, an open-voiced excuse for vice, the beginning of the century and not the end of it.

. 　 . 　 . 　 . 　 . 　 .

When Jack said " the beginning of the century " it ended the argument. Jack himself is *fin de siècle.* I would not like him to know how quickly he won the argument by the last assertion. I am not supposed to know—from Jack's standpoint of femininity, my femininity—the exact meaning of the idiom " *fin de siècle.*" But I know Jack, know him better than he knows himself. He is a sort of

" proper impropriety "—very proper and very
—I must say it even if it is Jack—improper.

. . . . . .

It is a great mixture, if one has the cool
audacity, the *sang-froid* to live up to himself.
In the end of the century one makes a con-
venience of *convenances;* in the beginning
of it—Jack must have thought I was asking
a conundrum when I said——

. . . . .

Now I'm sure I would not have launched
into such an argument if Jack had not been
away so long. Somehow my—it is what the
boys would call a system—my " system " with
Jack was out of practice. When he is away
I get into such a bad habit of having opinions.
And as he sat there with his head—that head
with its dissipated little glimmerings of gray
hair in among the black—back against the top
of the sleepy hollow, his feet, incased in the
immaculate patent leathers resting on the foot
cushions, his dinner coat thrown back on one
side for the tips of his fingers to rest in his
trousers pocket, his right hand holding the
" perfecto " as he puffed a cloud of smoke
into artistic rings—he did look so tired, so
burnt-out, I thought of those days he had

dropped out of sight with his nonchalant good-bye and his every-day greeting on coming back. It was almost involuntary when I said:

"Jack, what is the difference between a bohemian and a vagabond?"

He went on mentally counting the smoke rings and then said:

"One is a loaferish gentleman and the other is a gentlemanly loafer."

. . . . . .

It was not encouraging for an argument; Jack's answers never are. My system having slipped its moorings by Jack's absence and my being a bit nettled at his no-answer answer, I actually went into a long dissertation on the difference as I viewed it. I said the vagabond, the so-called "bohemian," was one thing, and the real "bohemian," the man who could adapt himself to the place and situation in which he found himself, was another; that the vagabond knew no law that would interfere with his selfish, unprincipled freedom; that he veneered his faults and vices with the title "bohemian"; that he considered himself licensed to drink his friend's wine, to smoke his cigars, to love his friend's wife, and to slip through life without paying his bills, if

only he could write a book or a story, compose
an opera, stage a play, or have some little
claim to the world where brains count instead
of money. A real bohemian? I intimated
that a true bohemian was somewhat my ideal
of a man.

.   .   .   .   .   .

Then Jack changed his position. He
lighted a fresh cigar and I knew that he was
preparing to clinch something. And then it
was that I came back to my " system " and remembered that Jack was Jack; that I never
argue with Jack. He is sufficient with me
unto himself, one of the few men I would not
want to convince, or to have weak enough to
be convinced by a woman if once his opinion
was formed. But there I was—launched!
And I was not going to tumble out of the
boat and wade ashore. I must ride back to
safety somehow.

.   .   .   .   .   .

I tried to insinuate or to give the impression that Jack himself was a real bohemian.
He puffed away at his cigar and listened without comment as I floundered through honor
and refinement and all that is best and truest
in men not necessarily being a matter of en-

vironment and conventionality; that companionship might make a man seek even the "sawdust and beer" if there, among the coterie of brilliant journalists, authors, artists and musicians, actors and diplomats and others, were men who could not afford the luxury of velvet carpets and champagne; that men, real men, might feel sometimes that they were stifled by conventionality; that it was only in this bohemia where one could dare to allow half-formed thoughts and theories to expand into something that could be met by the intellectual sparks that lie around loose even in the vagabondism of it.

.   .   .   .   .   .

As Jack still said nothing I took courage and enlarged on the charm of an atmosphere where rules were not laid down and where honor was honor and innate truths were not hidden, and that to the real bohemian decency, respectability and high principles were never lost sight of.

Then it was that Jack knocked the ashes from his cigar and took his inning. He said there never was, never will be a bohemia. It was simply a book, a play, that had been written and then staged in the early part of the

century; that its vices were so cleverly put
that ever since certain classes had been trying
to imitate and to live the play, but they always
failed, dismally and ignominiously; that it
was all intangible, and the only thing substantially recognized that had come out of it
was the excuse for vice and for the faultiest
faults; that there were no dividing lines in vice
or in respectability, and that, in short, bohemia
was obsolete.

.   .   .   .   .   .

I flatter myself that I am a good listener—
it was really the only way to get out of the
difficulty gracefully. Jack is really quite eloquent. His voice is deep and musical, and by
the time he was through I had listened so at-
tentively that he in his vanity was not sure
whether it was he or I who started the argument.

I am glad Jack is back again. It will keep
my wits sharpened up to have him about.

XII.

Really, for an up-to-date man Jack does fall below the line at times. I would enjoy telling him the difference between the "tiresome girl" and the "fascinating woman." But it would never do.

. . . . . .

He says he likes a "brilliant, clever, fascinating woman." To let him have a glimpse, however, of this cleverness, the cleverness that analyzes and sifts and convinces that your knowledge of life and of men and women is real, would make him wary, and I am thinking he would skip back to these self-same "tiresome girls" that in these end-of-the-century times are being relegated to rear seats.

A man—a man like Jack—keeps the "tiresome girl" guessing, and the "fascinating woman" keeps a man guessing. That's the difference.

. . . . . .

Men of Jack's kind act a part with the "tiresome girl" and get tired; the "fasci-

nating woman "—to myself I will say it—acts
a part and does not get tired.

.   .   .   .   .   .

And yet—really and truly—I am almost
afraid to think it—there are times when I
would like to break away from myself and fly
into Jack's arms—I should think my cheeks
would burn to acknowledge it, even to myself
—throw my arms around his neck, feel his
strong arms clasping me to his heart and his
sweet, strong kisses on my face—— (Gracious! How my face burns! I must be awfully demoralized to feel and think these impulses.) And what do I do instead?

.   .   .   .   .   .

It is all Jack's fault—I wonder if he knows
it! Of course since that day, since the time
a few weeks ago that Jack told me that he—
since the day that he asked me to marry him.
I presume both of us have been acting a part.
I have, and, why, surely, so has Jack—I know
it!

.   .   .   .   .   .

Jack in his wickedness—worldly wickedness—wanted a shrine. He would put me
on a pedestal—me! with all my experience
and experiences; the child-love with its dead

sorrow, the woman-love with its living sorrow,
Under-the-Grass a sacred memory, Over-the-
Grass a—a—well, a memory—the memory, I
suppose, that makes me "fascinating."

.   .   .   .   .   .

Jack and the men at the club placed me on
this pedestal because I defended Over-the-
Grass as long as I possibly could, refusing to
believe that he was away with that woman.
I said it privately and I said it to the reporters
in all that horrible time. Jack knew and the
others knew that I knew differently. But
must not a wife defend her husband and give
him a chance? So a shrine was created.
When Jack saw there were others as well as
himslf to give me great friendship at least, he
precipitated himself into an anxious lover in
place of the calm friend he had been for years,
and I could not lose my friend. I could not
afford to allow myself to soften into the nature that can be so tortured with love and the
suffering that seems so great a part of it. I
have had enough of it. I would not commit
myself.

.   .   .   .   .   .

Jack saw his mistake when the answer was
not forthcoming. In trying to obliterate from

my mind the turbulent love undercurrent that
can rush through the heart of a man like himself Jack has fallen back into the old way he had
when Over-the-Grass and he were chums and
I was "the wife of his friend." Jack was
then, as now, a man of honor. Whatever he
sets himself to do he does. But the holding
of himself in such a sphinx-like reserve has
been at times almost maddening—to me.

    .   .   .   .   .

Does he love me? Do I want him to? I
don't know. When he told me of it that day
I did not want to hear it. There are times
now when I do want to hear it. I liked
him then and I wanted him near me, but I
could not say yes, would not say no. He
grasped the situation and here we are, good
friends, "good fellows;" I "fascinating," as
he says, and he fascinating to the extent that
sometimes I actually long for him to say again
in the maddest way that he loves me. But
not Jack! He is too wise.

    .   .   .   .   .

I wonder if he will ever know how he has
made my heart thump when he has looked at
me steadily with those cool, dark gray eyes
and with that searching, never-off-guard way

of his? Some time I am morally certain I
shall break away and fly at him and devour
him with kisses—my heart quickens now in
thinking of it.

.   .   .   .   .   .

What do I now? Let me see; I look back
at Jack coolly as long as I dare, and then, still
coolly, I sometimes hand him a lighted parlor
match for his dying cigar. Once I had the
audacity——

.   .   .   .   .   .

It was at dinner. We had been chatting and
lingering over the dinner in that happy, contented, diamond-cut-diamond way we have
with each other. Jack had seemed to be several times on the verge of saying personal
things. He had enlarged to quite an extent,
for him, on the subject of girls and women.
It was easy enough to keep the conversation a
general one, but one cannot always keep
glances from being personal. And really it
had taken a good deal of tact to keep the subject general. Jack seemed trying to balance
the parrying with those direct looks of his.
It was all delightful, though my heart did take
a swirl and a swish with my nerves every few
minutes. But I smiled and chatted indiffer-

ently until, finally, as that awful impulse came sweeping over me, I, with a self-daring little laugh, raised my glass of champagne with that little toast :

"Here's to the wings of love!
May they never lose a feather
Until——"

Then, just then, a gleam shot into Jack's eyes and his half-raised glass was placed on the table and he interrupted me with :

"Take care, child, or I will take you in my arms and hold you there until you give me that answer you have withheld so long."

Here was an object-lesson of two hearts beating as one.

.   .   .   .   .   .

What did I do? I looked at Jack rather coolly and touched my foot to the electric button under the dining-table for the black coffee.

And it is these little things that make up the sum of "fascinations" in women for men

But really I could not exist without Jack. If he is wise, however, he will never let me understand how much he cares for me. If he does, his greatest fascination for me will be gone.

XIII.

It is the daintiness of women that rivets and enchains men—the perfume of the hair, the baby smell of the skin, the laces, the frills, the arched foot, diaphanous stuffs, clinging drapery—anything and everything that is delicate feminine luxury and entirely beyond them; added as an after thought, but coming first in reality, it is symmetry in form and the grace that is so essentially feminine. Awkwardness disenchants, and well-poised, graceful lines will hold forever.

.   .   .   .   .   .

There must, of course, be some brains, but the understanding of all these things means brain. It means a lot more that I don't care to go into argument about with anyone but myself; truly, I believe that summed up it means—this appreciation of all that is daintiest, of all that is most delicately effeminate in women—that it means purity to men, the purity of passion itself.

.   .   .   .   .   .

To be so essentially feminine places a woman

in the holy of holies in a man's heart. It
came to me with such force when Jack finally
spoke of "The Bacchante." I came nearer
loving Jack then than ever before. It was
such a surprise. Really I had thought to sort
of fight it out with Jack when I placed my
pretty reproduction here in my den. If Boston would not have "The Bacchante," what
chance was there for me to convince the few
favored ones who drop in here that to me "The
Bacchante," the mother, the child, the poise,
the exquisite outline, the grace, was the symbolism of purity, the God-given purity of
life?

．　　．　　．　　．　　．　　．

I reverenced you, you dear thing, and I felt
that I could reverence your creator, or anyone
who could in his higher cultivation weed out
all there is in humanity that appeals to the
coarser element and give us this divine purity
in the nude. The child suggests no greater
innocence than these outlines and the unconscious grace of the mother. You are life—
sacred and holy. I placed you there a bit in
the shadow, not because I would not defend
you, but because I dreaded ignorance—the ignorance that might criticise you and robe

you with the evil that can exist in the
mind.

.   .   .   .   .   .

Jack discovered you as he sank back in the
easy-chair.   He said nothing, but he looked
at you long and thoughtfully.   I studied his
face and wondered if when he spoke I would
hate him.   That is what it would have meant if
he could not see in you what I saw.   And yet
I felt that I could not expect it—he a man of
the world with full knowledge of life not as
it should be, but as it is.   He could not come
through fires of experience with the untainted
soul that could recognize all that is most up-
lifting in nature and in art, with the discrim-
ination and the understanding of all that is
most beautiful in nature and that what is God-
given must be pure—it would take the soul of
a saint in a man.   Not Jack, surely.

.   .   .   .   .   .

I waited for his comment.   I knew it would
come.   My thoughts flew away to that clergyman in the West who is at present criticis-
ing the Government and recognizing only ob-
scenity—and bringing it to the notice of his
congregation—in the partially nude figures of
beautiful women on the new silver certificates.

He says that the eye teaches the mind to remember and feed on vice. While I felt con-
tempt and knew that it was only the mind of
the reverend doctor that needed draping, I
did not want to be disappointed in Jack. He
looked so long, so earnestly, so thoughtfully,
that I finally became uncomfortable. Was he
disappointed in me? Was he not, after all,
going to give me an opportunity to defend
my dainty antique?

.   .   .   .   .   .

I would not argue with Jack. One thing
was sure: my pretty bronze should stay and
Jack could go. I could wait no longer. I
said:

"Well, Jack?"

"It is purity itself." I could feel the tears
somewhere near my eyes. "It is divine—what
more so than that this mother with her child
should be presented in such perfect outline,
without a suggestion of lewdness or vulgarity?
The pity of it is that it should even have had
the mantle of discussion thrown around it.
Another sin is that it should be perforce
viewed by people so ignorant and so mentally
debased that they can see only reason to blush
and to demand protection for public morals.

Such people are the ones who demoralize. They would drape pure cold marble and explain the reason to an innocent and unconscious child. It is the exquisite daintiness in 'The Bacchante' that should appeal to all that is best in men. It is God's most perfect creation perfected by the touch of art, and should teach the lesson of something higher and better than ourselves."

. . . . . .

It was a long speech for Jack, and I do not remember it all in its exactness, but—I did not hate Jack. And somehow all the evening I felt and recognized the grand strength of his manhood, and how men like him can worship women who are essentially feminine, delicate and dainty and needing the protection that is to them the first law of masculine nature. Women who never discover it are idiots.

. . . . . .

So, my dainty bronze, I am glad I bought you. You do more than gladden my eye. You made me forget all my "systems" with Jack, and for one evening made me earnest and honest, and you discovered to me that the souls of saints can exist even in men of the world.

XIV.

I believe that I am tired of everything—
everything real and everything unreal.

A year has gone by, now, since Over-the-
Grass became tangled, or tangled himself, in
the meshes of vice and a woman. Here by
myself I can acknowledge some mistakes I
made. Mistakes? Yes, they were most serious mistakes.

.   .   .   .   .   .

In an hour I must dress for my first real
" social " evening. I will throw myself in
among the pillows for the sixty minutes and
think it out. To begin with, I have been,
from the social standpoint, exceedingly proper.
Of course, there've been Jack and Reta and
Adelaide and Tom and the Major and others,
and suppers and dinners and life, but society
in its cold, critical generalism, has been barred
out.

There had to be a year of mourning—
mourning without the *crepe*. It was not respect to an honored dead, but respect to self-

respect, with no bid for public sympathy.

.   .   .   .   .   .

Sympathy from outsiders may be backed with the purest intentions, but it says plainly that you are getting the worst of something. I was not getting the worst of it. The sorrow was mine in its deepest humiliation, but Over-the-Grass was and would be getting the worst of it. I had not offended any code of honor, conscience or society. I tried to save him and he would not be saved. Afterward I defended him to give him one more chance; the defense was, to be sure, only a straw, but I realized his need of it. If a man has not the common sense to pay respect, at least outwardly, to social codes, there comes a time when he will be forced to recognize them. It was pity for his blindness—not, at the last, love for him—that compelled me to hold out the straw for him to clutch at. While the sweet sympathy of friends, the inner consciousness of right, make my position secure, though affairs of the heart will always seem insecure, there is a full realization of those mistakes I made.

.   .   .   .   .   .

I should have used my "systems" with Over-the-Grass as with other men. It is only since this year of retirement commenced that I have had the time to study out the real value of systems.

.   .   .   .   .   .

I would not use that word "system" with anyone but myself. I would soften it into that word that is used to signify that greatest of all social accomplishments—tact. System is a little private vulgarism, but it is what tact is—a studied method that is needed in the successful fitting of corners or in filling in when corners will not fit.

.   .   .   .   .   .

To be successful one must have systems or else be stupidly pretty; men are afraid of notoriously smart women. I do not flatter myself that I am exceptionally brilliant, but I ought to know men—twice married, two "pasts"—a dead and a living one—and I should have played systems with the living one as I did to some extent with others.

A stupidly pretty woman, illiterate, but with an animal instinct of shrewdness, made him forget honor, home and country. I lost him through cleverness and honesty, the hon-

esty and, perhaps, vanity that made me parade
for his admiration my keen insight into his
own nature, as well as into that of others. It
was not always flattering to him; neither was
it restful.

.   .   .   .   .   .

With a clever woman a man is constantly on
guard and proportionately uncomfortable. A
woman, to be successful, must be a comfort.
If she is unfortunate enough to be actually
clever she should cultivate a system—unselfish, unpretentious accomplishments that will
at times allow the inner nature of a man to
come to the surface for a glimpse of sunlight
and not be frightened back again before it has
its airing. If he thinks her cleverness will
analyze, dissect, criticise and sum up, he at
times gets shaky and weak-kneed, and immediately longs for another atmosphere.

.   .   .   .   .   .

This inner self may show up one way or
another, for good or for bad. It is a comfort
to the man when the woman is not smart
enough to discover or believe anything other
than what he for the time being wishes her to
know. Sometimes he is struggling for recog-
nition of his own brilliancy, and it annoys

him to have a woman in the race. He may win laurels through her, but he is the last to give her credit for having placed the wreath on his brow. If he is truly great, then he needs a woman with whom he can relax his brain tension.

Men somehow, too, never attribute to a really smart woman any nice sense of honor. If she be endowed with any particular intelligence and he discovers it with capable ability, he is prone to think that she must necessarily be a "schemer," and unless he knows her very well he will class her among that unenviable list of "adventuresses" which at once covers the whole gamut of wickedness. To him a woman cannot be honorable and smart, too; honor, brilliancy and glittering achievements need the strength of a man.

  . . . . . .

But with a system life is smooth sailing. Its first principle is not to betray decided opinions. If one has an opinion it must be made to appear to come from him. And then one must be dainty, clinging and effeminate. He will never connect keen insight and understanding of foibles and intelligent ability with feminine frippery, for the reason that the so-called clever woman despises these trifles, which to her signify feminine weakness. She is supposed to dress—and it is really, for the rest of us. very thoughtful on her part—like a man as much as possible, or with crooked hats and straggling hair and with utter forgetfulness of such an unimportant thing as looks. She can stalk through life in her own chosen way, and your man, the best and the worst, is on guard against her. But the system with its merry laughing, chatter and banter, never argumentative, never rubbing the fur the wrong way, never unbelieving, never seeing through a sham, never forgetting a frill or a flounce or a frippery, brings you always safely to shore.

.   .   .   .   .   .

No, my dear, dear self, systems are positively necessary. They may at times tire you and make you feel that life is an effort and that things real are as uninteresting as the unreal, but it will not hurt you to flatter and be sweetly amiable and non-committal. If I had to try it over again—no, if I had studied systems as much before this past year as since—I would not have been so honest with Over-the-Grass. If I had to be honest and real at times

I might have tried it on some other fellow—
Jack perhaps. But now it is Jack on whom I
am trying these experiments and——

What is that! Time to dress? Have I
been here an hour? Really, thinking things
over is interesting.

XV.

Ah, you and I again, my pretty den!
A whole week without an hour with you.
A week? Can it be possible? A week of
what? Society and monuments.

.   .   .   .   .   .

You and I in these reveries—here in the
mellowness of shaded lamps, firelight, draperies, cushions and indolent luxury—sometimes
open graves; but we do not run up against
cold, unyielding monuments. Society, my
own lovely, protecting den, is full of monuments.

.   .   .   .   .   .

It is only a week since I again began the
swirl of it. One day has followed another
with its hours—and its hours reaching far into
the night—filled with the old familiar routine,
the old life as it was before Over-the-Grass—
when Over-the-Grass was a part of it. It is
all the same, the surface of it, but the line of
monuments—I don't mind whispering it here
in my den—the monuments are a cold, hard,
glaring white; Over-the-Grass everywhere, at

every turn, standing there, a shadow between the past and present, reminding me of the life that is dead and of the vague emptiness, the aimless—I'll not think of it.

Here's to you, Bacchante, Phryne and the firelight, in this sip of tea—we do not run up against cold monuments here in this dainty den, that remind one constantly that there is a lot of desolation in aftermath.

.   .   .   .

Of course, Jack and the rest have not known of these mental reflections—Heaven forbid! —in this week of gayety. Jack says I carry myself well, that he is proud of me—as much as he dares to be—and then he added that my greatest charm for him and for those who know me best is my naturalness.

.   .   .   .

And is that what I am—natural? Natural! —with all these suppressed impulses! You and I, my dear self, consider that rather far-fetched—do we not?

.   .   .   .

Am I ever natural? When I laugh? Yes. It is, most of the time, such a huge joke. Being non-committal is so foreign to my every impulse. It was an experiment at first and

surely was good discipline. What was I, anyhow? Of so little account that any kind and
all kinds of women walked off with my husband. To be sure he came back—came back
too late. Most things in this life are too
late.

.   .   .   .   .   .

In my latent realization of my own lack of
fascination—I had been in my egotism looking upon myself as paramount—I commenced
to be politic and tactful. It teaches one un-
selfishness. It teaches the art of drawing out
and studying other people — yourself un-
studied. It teaches the accomplishment of
conforming the circles in your own nature to
the square corners in the make-up of others.
You learn not to be pedantic in talking. You
learn to be epigrammatic. You make, of
course, your epigram fit the didactic state-
ment of your listener and you get a reputation
for wit and for having a keen appreciation of
humor—a rare quality in women.

.   .   .   .   .   .

Jack says my being natural—I can't help
the smile—frank and unaffected in every way,
creates surprise, because with it I am such a
woman of the world—that I am the two ex-

tremes, a woman of knowledge and at the same time as innocent and outspoken as a child.

.   .   .   .   .   .

It seemed at first a doubtful compliment. Then as he went on and said my knowledge made me interesting and my innocence made me a woman, a baby to be petted, I commenced to be glad and sorry, too, that I was a woman —glad for the love of it, sorry for the sorrow of it.

.   .   .   .   .   .

If women could only outgrow the child part of their natures, hearts would not bleed so much. One of the greatest surprises in life is to discover how much sorrow the heart can bear, how much it can ache, how it can be strained to the utmost, crowded with agony, and yet not break.

.   .   .   .   .   .

As Jack went on I realized the beauty and truth of that phrase, "It is not how much a woman knows, but how she knows it." Jack and Over-the-Grass and the rest of the clique are good teachers. In making me a chum they have made me in the world, but not of it. They have taught me to understand, observe and make just and sensible deductions as an observer, and thus escaping the prejudices of a participator. Though, goodness knows, I have had participation—more than most women —matrimonially.

.   .   .   .   .   .

When a second "past" looms up, a woman cannot disclaim personal experience, particularly when in the passing it leaves a living sorrow that is worse than the dead one. It is the living sorrow and not the dead one that lines up the monuments in your social pathway even after a whole year of retirement. The dead one brings desolation, but—there I am again with the monuments and thinking of the strangeness of the social round without Over-the-Grass. I cannot seem to get away from it. I wonder if the end of it all—I——

.   .   .   .   .   .

Tears!!! Well, my dear, natural self, I am ashamed of you. I shall go out of my den, and close the door and get away from you. You have no sense, no pride. You are a disappointment. Go back to your "systems" and try them first on yourself. Let others think you natural, but don't make the mistake of being so.

.   .   .   .   .   .

XVI.

Bacchante, you are the symbolism of purity, and Phryne, you are exquisite physical perfection, but, alive, you would be but a small part of existence—of love. You might appeal to some ideals in a man, but he would tire of you. You would, I imagine, if endowed with the warmest life, finally be nothing more to him than the pictures on the wall or as you are now, the statuary that pleases the artistic sense. If you were uncertain in some way—a care, an anxiety, a——

.   .   .   .

Who is it says that life's comforts are its cares, that if one has not cares he must make them or be wretched, that care is employment and action, a joy? And so it is with love. Life and love must have employment and action. There must be responsibility and a striving for something to make either endurable, enduring or comforting.

.   .   .   .

When a man is very young he worships an ideal and consumes his love to dead ashes in

gratifying his senses. Raking over the ashes
of the numerous bonfires he has made of his
senses, he finds a revelation of his inner self.
He recognizes his weaknesses, his unworthiness. He wants something better than he has
known—not in others but in himself. He discovers a spot of tenderness in his soul that
has remained untouched.

. . . . . .

A man's heart—presuming for the moment
that the heart is really the centre of these
emotions—is only a part of the digestive
organs; it needs variety in equal doses to be
healthy and perfectly normal. It gets dys-
pepsia because he sections off the varieties and
takes each part by itself. He takes the sweets
in his youth and keeps the senses burning at
high flame and finds that his better self has
been starving. He must have the employment, the earnestness, the care, the striving
for something in his love that will develop
and satisfy the unselfish part of himself that
has not had its innings.

. . . . . .

It is the same with women.

. . . . . .

This is moralizing, and smacks of senti-

ment, but it is nature—after you get ac-
quainted with it.

.   .   .   .   .   .

Adelaide is responsible for this train of
thought. Now, there's a woman a man should
worship with all his senses and with all the
dormant tenderness that he hides in his heart.
If I were a man I would—I do love her, but
I have wished that she were a man—well,
now, what is it I wish? I think it is this:
that I knew a man who understands himself
as she understands herself and who could
awaken in me and bring into action every fibre
of my intellect, ambition, tenderness, honesty
and best self as she does. It would be love
with the fulfilment of all that is human. Ah,
my friend, all that is lacking is that you are
a woman. This friendship can come but once
in a lifetime. Your strength and your glorious womanhood have a way of unfolding all
that is dormant in my nature, and in my reverence for you I want to be all that you would
have me. To be my best self, to garner some
sheaves, I need your companionship. No man
has ever created or developed this in me. So
I say if you were a man there could be com-
pleteness in love. My " care " and " joyous

action " has been what I have striven for others to do.

For yourself, you are all that a man worships in his very young senses, and all that he would strive to attain, to work for, to hold with his noblest and manliest and most steadfast purpose. And yet you write to me—it is this letter of yours that has started this moralizing.

You write that you must have action in its deepest sense ; your accomplishments, as an inward resource, are but trifling pleasures. You tell me that you knew exactly what my opinion would be of your future plans and that you are sorry I do not encourage you. Months ago your mind was settled upon it, only the time to begin was shadowy ; that did you not do it you would perhaps be in mischief or unhappy ; that you are looking at life seriously and earnestly ; that without this real work the things you would take up would not call forth the best in yourself ; that you must have bookwork and study to make you forget everything—"all the years of lost good !"

You tell me that you realize all that I— who am " so keen in sympathy because of your

fine delicate nature "—portray to you, but
that you do not think yourself very sympathetic, that while I creep into everybody's
heart and life, you draw only those whose
orbit you have in your plane; that it
would not do for me to take up a science of
this kind, but that you have always felt inclined in this direction. If it should prove a
failure your time will not have been lost because you are gaining in knowledge of yourself, of the world at large.

.   .   .   .   .   .

Adelaide, your words cut like a knife when
you say how well you realize the sacrifice and
the work just when you could enjoy life at its
fullest, but that, even if you fail, you will have
gained a victory over yourself in being able to
set aside your own pleasure for the good you
may and can do others. I blush for my own
idleness and aimlessness. You will go on and
not fail; I will go on and be as you left me
—with the despair at times you speak of and
at the slightest business worry or complica-
tion, saying : "Oh, dear, what shall I do ?—
any kind of a husband is better than none at
all ! "

.   .   .   .   .   .

I blush for my own frittering away of the

hours, but, dear heart, I feel your presence as
I read what you say about dropping into my
den for one of our talks; that the memory
of them will be the refreshing bits in your
career of study and work and bring the stim-
ulant of relaxation and lift you out of rigid
discipline.

. . . . . .

So, Bacchante and Phryne and my idle self,
we are not exactly failures. We seem to be
filling some kind of a niche. I think I will
dress for dinner, and, in some way, try to
make Jack understand that I am a "care," or
that he is not awakened to his best self, or
that action—or that he—I—well, anything to
pass away the evening.

XVII.

"Merry Christmas is bathed alike in sunshine and in storm," and life is a colossal joke
—after the passing of the sunshine and storm,
and in the summing up of the pranks Fate
plays with it.

.   .   .   .   .   .

A den is a cosy, luxurious nook at night in
the light of the shaded lamps and firelog; but
at this hour that is neither of day nor night,
in the fading of the one and before the coming of the other, sentiment and rose-color take
on a cold, practical grayness. Why did I
wander in here at this hour, when colors cannot be seen by either candle-light or day?

.   .   .   .   .   .

Those pillows over there in that shadowy
couch corner that are so restful, tempting and
beautiful in color scheme in the glow of evening light, are dull and repellant. This statuary—really, Bacchante and Phryne, I don't
know but that the enterprising friend of public morals is right; perhaps you do need

clothes—you look cold. This easy-chair by the window, with the curtains half-drawn, has a melancholy atmosphere pervading it as if someone had been counting the straggling, falling snowflakes and measuring by them life's anniversaries. These ashes scattered here on the rug have fallen from a listless hand that held a cigar with its sparks slowly dying; Jack must have set down here to wait for me. I wonder if he, too, felt the grayness, and, while he waited, counted the years backward from the Christmas time that comes faithfully, no matter what else fail.

.   .   .   .   .   .

Christmas is the never-forgotten calendar of the heart. With it comes, involuntarily, the pacing backward from year to year the events of our lives, the study of the inner self, and all the embroidered surfaces. The sunshine and the shadow, evenly divided, mark the years as they have flitted by; sunshine, the eager, joyous anticipation of childhood and the happier reality of the mysterious visits of Santa Claus; shadow, the home circle broken and the despair that finds no comfort.

.   .   .   .   .   .

It was your first lesson in living that life

could slip away from a loved one and leave you living on, never to know the same unalloyed happiness again. It was the sorrow of a child, and the slipping away into eternity of the life of a brother; but no love since has been so unselfish, so perfect. It was between you a silent sympathy, a thought commenced in the one and finished by the other, a faith unbounded, an understanding without words or explanations, each with the same joys, same sorrows, enhanced or lessened because of each other—each the other half of each other's soul.

.   .   .   .

Life snapped suddenly for him and closed down the covers of the book for you. Other Christmases, other joys came, but those before were a part of an unbroken past; those since have had their joys marked with chasms.

.   .   .   .   .   .

Years and Christmas have galloped on faster and faster. Love and death have come again. There has been death in life, death in love and life in death. Life, love and death have danced their jig with you, and death in life, too, has left a trail of darkness that made blank the present; but the halo around the chasm in your memory-castle that blocked the pathway of that unbroken past tells you the chasm could not be so deep had not that past been so laden with sunshine.

. . . . . .

When once life's lessons begin they go on, pace by pace, in a mad rush of events. Fate twists and turns and twirls you through and around human follies and treachery. It laughs at you, and the sorrow of it all is that you bat up against all that is false, with all that is true in yourself until there is such a *potpourri* of sunshine and storm gathered around you that neither is worth the effort of cultivating or of escaping.

. . . . . .

And so, sitting here in the gray twilight, with the dead flecks of ashes on the rug and the snow falling faster now, with occasional half-frozen flakes beating against the window-glass, I find life a huge joke, a farce-comedy. With my heart alive to beautiful child-life, with a panorama passing mentally of the two "pasts"—Under-the-Grass and Over-the Grass —with full realization of the desolation in a solitary life, I ought to be pacing up and down the floor holding my hands to high

heaven for consolation. And what am I doing? Smiling.

.   .   .   .   .   .

I am smiling and I am not unhappy. I
have nothing to make me miserable. Batting
up against the extremes of happiness and misery was awfully wearing. It really makes
one look worried and uninteresting. It is
much better to pass through the storm of both
and settle down into a condition, where you
appreciate the comedy of it all. My only real
worriment now is the perplexing thought that
comes to me : how would it have been if I had
been the aggressor and had been the one to
lead Fate's dance with the other fellow? I
can afford to smile at the grimness of it all,
because I was really conscientious. If any
wrong-doing of mine had been added to the
suffering that came to me, the joke would be
flat. I was not, during those years, particularly
in sympathy with the sentiment of virtue having its own reward ; still I am glad that it has
—the reward must be the ability to understand philosophically these little jokes.

.   .   .   .   .   .

The sorrows and the anguish that come
with the closing down of the coffin lid making

the "only rank in nature capacity for pain" have a sweet tenderness that keeps the heart alive and open to more suffering. The sorrows that toss you about, the living ones—if you just get enough of them—teach you conclusively what happiness is; that it is not being in abject misery.

.   .   .   .   .   .

In this Christmas time in the gray twilight of my den, miles away from all that tore my heart into shreds last Christmas time, with the storms of love, pride and misery all passed away, I can smile at Fate and defy it to take another turn with my tears.

XVIII.

Dear! dear! New York is woefully small,
and the path of our own particular orbit sur-
prisingly narrow—under a flashlight photograph; I wonder what next?

. . . . . .

Jack said I must cultivate women. It has
been restful not to exert myself in that way
recently. But Jack, in his masterful way, with
no room for argument, took the matter in
hand, and said that women, and women only,
could carry me safely over all social reefs.
He intimated that I was sure to be a favorite
with men, and if I would make myself agreeable to women—of course women with husbands and assured social positions—that the
Over-the-Grass past would not stand in the
way of my being a success, now that I was
alone. He said men were willing to admire,
praise and protect women whom they respected, but that they were also moral cowards, and followed, too, where women lead, and

that women controlled what is designated as
" society."

.   .   .   .   .   .

When I forgot my usual caution with Jack
and betrayed worldly wisdom by hinting that
women—some of them—were more to be
dreaded as friends than as enemies, that the
women who were at present recognized as
the most powerful social leaders, were possibly busy with private intrigues and would
have no interest in me, he interrupted me
and said that if I would unbend to them a
bit—even to some of these old friends of
Over-the-Grass—he would see that I was met
more than half way.

.   .   .   .   .   .

I did as Jack suggested. I made myself
charming, particularly to Mame and Evelyn,
They are surely a power socially, and my
knowing Tom so well, Jack made a specialty
of my cultivating Mame; though he himself
has never chanced to meet Tom, he said it
was not good form for me to receive gentlemen unless I was on visiting terms with their
wives. For some reason that I could not
fathom he was also anxious for me to take up
Evelyn. When I said I could not very well

make advances, as she was almost a stranger.
he said he would take care of that, and he
did; Evelyn called the next day. Evidently
men too have private wires of their own.

.   .   .   .   .   .

I really wore myself out being "agreeable,"
and here I am stranded, with it all to do over
again with other satellites—if this thing becomes known—thanks to modern science and
theatrical souvenir nights.

.   .   .   .   .   .

Of course the Casino management was
right in thinking a flashlight photograph of
the audience would make a pleasing souvenir.
It would at all times please some of the audience, but never at any time please all of it.

.   .   .   .   .   .

Ye gods! It showed as much rustic sense
in the manager as it did provincialism in
Mame and Evelyn's idea of a "night off."
When Mame told Tom that she must go to
Boston to visit her dear, neglected mother and
with tears and kisses said the only tug was
leaving him, such a darling husband, for four
days, she probably meant it. The tears could
have been genuine; it must have hit her conscience to have him stuff the big roll of money

into her hand and tell her to have a good time. Women always have consciences. Conscience is the twin of selfishness, but one never interferes with the other; one sleeps while the other works. If her conscience while it was working had subdued her vanity a bit, Tom would not now be tearing his hair. When he remarked that the lovely black-and-white striped satin dress was rather a "howling affair" for the train, she should have changed it. Such big things hang on such little trifles!

.   .   .   .

How these sleeves in their conspicuous stripes do stand out on each side of the programme with which she takes the precaution to cover her face! But for those rich and elegant stripes, not suitable for a railroad train, but *comme il faut* for the carriage and theatre, Tom would never have recognized in the picture the companion of Evelyn's husband—his own wife, whom he supposed was *en route* for Boston that evening. Then Tom in his devotion to newspapers, family and social morals, in scanning the rest of the picture to see if there were any more faces concealed behind programmes, discovers Evelyn! Evelyn with her face partially covered accompa-

nied by a gentleman unknown to him, and
apparently blissfully unconscious that a few
rows back of her sits her husband with her
dearest friend! Gracious! What is an X-ray
compared with a flashlight!

. . . . . .

Tom is dancing jigs—moral ones. He has
gone to Boston. I ought to have gone, too,
to tell Mame that I could have been there myself that night—with Tom! Tom said we could
go to the Casino and to the Waldorf to supper
without unpleasant comment from the "tab-
bies," because at the former the play had
been running so long that we would not meet
any of the town people and at the latter we
would be shielded by the palms from being
too conspicuous or would join some friends,
making a party. There was no harm in going
with dear old Tom in his loneliness, but I was
doing the heavy agreeable to Tom's wife and
did not like to mix things and chances of being cut off from Mame's invitation list. There's
no doubt about virtue bringing its own reward
this time.

. . . . . .

It is a laughable social mixture. The most
amusing part of this enlarged double-paged

newspaper cut is the unconsciousness of Evelyn and her swagger husband, of each other's presence. I wonder if it is these peccadilloes of his that made Jack at one time call him a cad ?

. . . . . .

Tom in his moral jig danced in here, wild with the deceit he has discovered. He glared at me because I could see no difference between Mame going with Evelyn's husband and his going with me—it being only luck and worldly sense on my part that we had no been obliged to use programmes ourselves that night.

. . . . . .

He tore his hair a bit, too, it seemed to me, because he could not go to Evelyn for consolation. He appears overanxious to discover who it is with her. He said he took a magnifying glass to study the features, but it was no one that he knew. Her face is partially covered with the programme, but jolly Evelyn evidently considers it all a good joke, judging by the way her face is turned with a laugh toward her escort. Her husband looks about the color of Mame's programme in the unnatural light. Orchestra stalls are certainly not good places to hide from the stage flashlight.

.   .   .   .   .   .

I wonder, myself, who it is with Evelyn— it is very indistinct—can only distinguish a dress suit.   I will get a magnifying glass.

.   .   .   .   .   .

Good heaven !   It is Jack !

XIX.

Ah, my bronze Bacchante and marble
Phryne, you are missing a lot by not being
alive, but one does not commence to live
until—I was going to say until one is ready
to die, but that is not it.

. . . . . .

Life is one thing and illusions are another.
One does not begin to live until the passing of all illusions. The passing of illusions
is despair and death only when you are not
capable of enjoying comedy. Life, as it really
is, is a farce comedy—if you can come up
from the depths of life's truths and be yourself a philosopher out of the pale of personal
emotion, and a " looker-on in Vienna."

. . . . . .

This last act in the comedy is great! The
curtain fell heavy and directly on my head,
when I discovered in the flashlight souvenir
picture, through the magnifying glass, that
Evelyn's escort was Jack. It was certainly a
surprise, but it was life—life as it is, and a
most enjoyable one. Illusions are wearing.

They bring extremes of happiness and of misery. They rend your soul. But life! Jolly life—if your experiences through illusions are volcanic enough to give you a philosophic after-balance—jolly, social life can keep mirth bubbling until sometimes you could throw up your hat in joy that you are in it, of it, and yet not of it.

.   .   .   .   .   .

The only serious drawback is that you must laugh alone. It would be so awkward to mention these mirthful trifles to other members of the farce-comedy. Personalities are so vulgar. Society, refined society, only deals in generalities.

.   .   .   .   .   .

Jack was wiser than I knew when he said that I must cultivate women. Of course it is true that women control society, and the study of social pathology is most interesting; but the marvelous depths of Jack's "systems" I was somewhat unprepared for, or I would not have been in the way of that aforesaid falling curtain.

.   .   .   .   .   .

Jack is a dear, good fellow. He knew just where to have me anchor my Over-the-Grass past. Mame and Evelyn are a power to assist, and evidently they would have been a rock that could also have blocked. Jack steered the boat. When he, like England's prince, signified the wish that a friend of his be called upon, and her name be placed on their exclusive invitation list, the same as before a great trouble came to her, it was done. This picture proves beyond all question that Jack had private wires of his own, and they chanced to be laid where he could use them for me to the best advantage.

.   .   .   .   .   .

Surely I am substantially launched. It needs now, on my part, only a level head. That my position is secure was evident at the ball last night. The surface of everything was the same as always—polished proprieties. The only thing particularly noticeable to me —and of course Jack's calm eagle eye noticed it, too—was the shade of *empressement* in Tom's manner to me. There were two or three reasons for it : First and foremost, of course, myself. But the interest was strengthened by his burst of confidence in bringing me the newspaper and telling me of the discovery he had made in recognizing a conspicu-

ous pair of sleeves on a pair of arms which
held a programme over a face—his wife's.
His wife with the husband of her friend
Evelyn! And then Evelyn! Evelyn down
in front with a man unknown to him. Of
course, I never told Tom of the discovery I
made after he had gone. And Tom never recognized Jack when he was introduced last
night—the features, fortunately, in that picture are so indistinct.

. . . . . .

The polished surface and the unconsciousness of some of the participants in the comedy
were very amusing. Tom, of course, is too
socially wise to mention to Mame the discovery
he made. Such things are reserved and fit
only for divorce courts. The four—Mame
and Evelyn's husband, Evelyn and Jack—undoubtedly scanned the souvenir photograph
prepared by theatrical management to see if
there was danger of an *exposé*. And they!
They are too serene, too elegant, too high up
the social ladder to cross lines and discuss or
attempt to explain. It would be very bad
form. Silence, on occasion, is not only golden,
but so aristocratic. It was all so astounding,
that only a flashlight photograph could have

convinced one that such fashionable *elegantes* could ever be found in unconventional pairs, in orchestra stalls, at an unfashionable play!

. . . . . .

Tom's interest in me may be for the present rather pleasant, but it is purely accidental and properly safe. It would not be socially safe to have one man noticeably interested. It is better to have several—unless it be some one like Jack.

. . . . . .

Dear Jack! I know his heart has not strayed even if he was in the compromising —ordinarily compromising—position of escorting another man's wife to the theatre without the protection of a "party." I know it by the jealous gleam in his eyes at Tom's attentions to me. But Jack must be punished a bit. I am not supposed to understand "systems." I don't know just how the punishment will come about—will let it take care of itself. I am anxious to see how cool, calm, debonair Jack will carry it out. It is not often now that one can catch him "off guard." He will come into the den for black coffee and his cigar. I will have the double-paged newspaper cut, lying where he can see it.

. . . . . .

It was great! I must throw myself down among the cushions to think it over. With his cigar lighted, Jack finally said, carelessly:

" Your friend Tom seems a fine fellow— have you known him long ? "

" Not so long, but intimately."

" Intimately ? It is strange I never met him until last night. May I ask what is the definition of intimately as you use it ? "

" He comes to me in trouble."

" Trouble ?" with perplexed and a gathering-storm emphasis.

" Yes, I answered, in a matter-of-fact manner, " domestic trouble."

" *Domestic* trouble!" and the cloud was black in Jack's face. To discuss private family affairs with an outsider is the blackest crime on the social calendar in Jack's eyes.

" Yes," I said, indifferently, and with almost a yawn.

" Comes to *you* to discuss his wife ? "

" Yes, sometimes," and I took a sip of coffee.

.   .   .   .   .   .

There was a time when Jack would have strode across the den in his earnestness, but since it has been diamond cut diamond between us, and a sort of crossing social swords in worldly wisdom, he seems to consider elegant nonchalance the better part. Still, Phryne, I think he really would have enjoyed smashing you, there was such jealous fury in his eyes. He took a long puff at his cigar and knocked off the ashes. Then he said, quietly, with a tinge of sarcasm:

"With your nice sense of honor it must be very annoying to you."

"Oh, no," with another sip of coffee, "I rather enjoy it."

"But you are recognized at present as a friend to his wife, and, pardon my presumption, though you have never given me my answer—you—are—my—intended wife."

"Am I? Well, I think I am a friend to his wife." I ignored the last part of his assertion, and then added, "he invited me to go to the theatre with him and I would not go."

"Invited *you* to go to the theatre with him! Did he think for one instant that you would go?"

Gracious! Jack forgot his careless drawl. His tone was actually vigorous.

"Yes, I think he did. Mame was, or he thought she was, on the way to Boston."

Jack's vigor was lost in a sigh and he said :

"My dear child, do I understand you? You have held yourself from such things, and you would not, I am sure, bring misery to another woman, and a man, married or not, cannot help loving you if he is——"

"Oh, it is not that," I interrupted; "you see, Jack. Tom loves Mame and he loves to talk about her, and he lets me see his good, pure love for her, and Mame—well, Tom's trouble was the flashlight photograph that was taken at the Casino (Jack started), and poor Tom recognized his wife's striped sleeves, and then he discovered Evelyn's husband—and—Evelyn—and——" Jack scarcely breathed. I adjusted the pillows a little more comfortably under the arm that was supporting my head and then said : " He brought me the enlarged picture in the newspaper lying there on the table."

.   .   .   .   .   .

For an instant Jack did not move. I sipped some more coffee, but it was cold. I rang for it to be removed. After it had gone Jack leisurely arose from the easy-chair, sauntered over to the table and took up the paper. He looked at the picture, and holding it in his hand said :

" A very fair reproduction."

And that was all he said.

. . . . . .

Ah, Jack, you are magnificent. I would have detested you if you had attempted an explanation.

XX.

Passing away is '97, my dear Marble
Phryne.

.   .   .   .   .   .

The stepping out of the old year and the
coming in of the new one matters little to us.
You and I haven't much to regret, and less
for which to hope. We now know the world
too well to go through it with hopes and dis-
appointments—and regrets?

.   .   .   .   .   .

Well, Phryne, that bowed head of yours on
your exquisitely moulded marble arm signifies
confusion and shame, but somehow it does not
suggest regret nor remorse. You are blushing
with shame, not because you have loved very
humanly, but because your accusers and judges
are viewing you with cold, critical eyes, and
not with those of love. It is not so much
what you, yourself, think that causes you to
cover your face, as it is what others think of
you. For yourself you loved, your soul awakened, you lived, you were only human, and
you do not regret. You study yourself, and

through your whole being there are thrills of
rejoicing; you do not regret because you are
too alive with love.

.   .   .   .   .   .

But, Phryne, my dear Marble Phryne, con-
fidentially, men are so different from women.
While women study themselves and rejoice
that they have lived and loved—"loved"
should come first; you live after her you love
—and blush only at censure; a man will study
himself individually and regret; he has regret
for things left undone and remorse for things
done. Why? Things in this world must be
balanced. There is no one, collectively, to
censure him because *he* has lived, so he cen-
sures himself. Sometimes his remorse is
whetted because he "lives" first and loves—
some other woman afterward.

.   .   .   .   .   .

Phryne, I don't think I like men who become consumed with remorse. Remorse is the
accompaniment of selfishness. A man will go
the pace, please every impulse, every desire,
strew his path with the tears of those who
love him, break someone's heart, then after
he has been "happy" he will awaken to the
fact that being "happy" is greatest misery.

He ought to study himself collectively, as it were, and live his life in self-approval—stand by his sins—if they are human ones—stand by his good deeds, and keep his moral book balanced, and not wash and rinse his conscience so often.

.   .   .   .

Throughout the year he takes these moral baths on occasion and then he doubles up sins and baths in the passing of the year, and welcomes the new year with deep-dyed remorse and resolutions.   He looks forward to the coming of the day January First with actual longing, because on that day he is going to be square with himself and the world.   In the meantime he takes his last drinks, his last cigars, his last game of cards, his last night out with " the boys," his last promiscuous kisses.   He doubles and trebles on these last adieus because the end is coming and this life is to know him no more.   He says good-by, royally and commences all over again.   He does the same each year.

.   .   .   .

Why?   Because he is either too good or too bad.   He goes to extremes.   His pleasure runs into follies that rack him physically, then his remorse sees only sin in pleasure. He tries to be good, and life becomes a burden because it has no spice. He takes at first a little spice, being human, and he gradually works around into the mixture again, and each new year finds him knocking in the same old way at resolution's door.

．　　　．　　　．　　　．　　　．　　　．

He is always a saint or a sinner. He knows no happy medium. If he could only make of the saint a human sinner and the sinner saint-seasoned, he would be more of a comfort to himself. He gauges all goodness in a man from the purity of boyhood.

．　　　．　　　．　　　．　　　．　　　．

He studies it out from memory's castle whose bells ring to him the sweetest in the coming of the new year. He does not remember so much the unconsciousness and the irre-sponsibilities of life, as it was then, as he does the joyousness of it all. The snow was whiter, the bells were merrier, the ice was smoother, the skates were sharper, cheeks were redder, girls prettier, the world better and was his be-cause he knew no sin. A little later, in man-hood's first flush, the world is really his if only handled conscientiously. After a while comes the love of association, and association is always whetted with slipping from the narrow paths, and a man cannot slip moderately. He must go to the end of the rope and feel its sudden jerk, then he brings himself together and faces his man—himself—that needs reforming.

.   .   .   .   .   .

But there must be a grand round-up if all these pleasures are to be relegated to the past. He enters with renewed zest into the dissipation and he afterward plunges the same way into goodness. He must have rest and peace, because he has so wearied of pleasure.

.   .   .   .   .   .

He will be good, Phryne, for some time after the ringing of the bells for '98. He will be good until the halo of goodness seems to him surrounded by midnight darkness. Then he will commence again the pace that will prepare him for resolutions and duties in the passing of '98.

XXI.

Phryne, dear, a Jersey judge and a passion poetess have been winding themselves up on the subject of kissing. The judge said it was disorderly conduct and the poetess said—she said a lot of things; among others that marriages were made or missed by it. She seems to offer condolence to the girl who " misses," and intimates that the calamity might have been averted if only the kiss—just one kiss— had been withheld! A bit severe, eh, Phryne?

.   .   .   .   .   .

By the way, my beautiful marble dear, why do I find myself talking—reverizing to you, more than to bronze Bacchante? Is it because history and art have made you seem more worldly-wise? As I look at you both in the glint of the firelight, your exquisite curves and outlines are equally perfect, equally pure ; but, Phryne, that bowed head of yours shows consciousness, and Bacchante, with her heaven-raised chin, is unconscious. Both of you have knowledge—in different ways. If I should talk to Bacchante about kisses—the

right or the wrong of them—her eyes would
open wide, startled at any question of wrong,
and my words would demoralize her.   I would
have to explain that there are those who discover wrong in things God-given and in
nature. I would not like that, Phryne ; I
would not like to destroy that innocent, unconscious pose. But you, Phryne? If I asked
you about kisses, and I could see your eyes,
you would half close them to conceal from me
how much you know, and you would not care
—you would not be convinced there was
wrong in anything so typical of love ; so,
naturally, you being as you are, and I—as I
am, there is spice in talking to you.

 . . . . . .

Now, what was it the poetess said ?—that
marriages were made and missed by the kiss,
and she concludes with the advice that it is
better to remain in the memory of a man as
the one woman whom he could not kiss, than
to be remembered among the many he has
kissed and forgotten. What do you and I
think about that, Phryne ?

 . . . . . .

Just between you and me, I believe I prefer
to be remembered by the kiss I gave, than by

the one I did not give. If he were the man
I could kiss, he would get a glimpse of my
soul, and if he could forget—then it were
better—a blessing, that the marriage missed.

.   .   .   .   .   .

But the poetess made a distinction between
the girl and the woman of the world. Her
theories were preconceived ones, coming out
of the dark ages, and are a perfectly safe code
of morals—for girls. A girl in her kisses
seeks her soul, a woman—if she loves—gives
her soul.

.   .   .   .   .   .

I am sure that Jack—it is bad form to be
personal, Phryne, even here by ourselves in
this little den—I am very certain that Jack
would never have remembered me so loyally
all this time but for that one glimpse—that
one kiss I gave him. It has held him because
of the glimpse, it has held him because of the
trust; he knew that I knew him, man of the
world that he is, and yet trusted him. It
placed him on a pedestal with himself—and
with me—and he has never stepped down
from it. He believes in himself, he believes
in me, and he is willing to wait—of course,
Phryne, there is a story about that kiss—it is

too sacred to even indulge in a revery about
it.

.   .   .   .   .   .

But there's a difference in men. As a class,
men of the nineteenth century are susceptible
to flattery and are also distrustful; two traits
that are not balanced with an iota of sense
where women are concerned. A man is susceptible to flattery because of a natural conceit. If he fails to win a kiss from a girl he
thinks "if I cannot kiss her no man can;" if
he succeeds then there is this incongruity—he
thinks "every man can."

.   .   .   .   .   .

One would think his vanity would stand by
him better than that. In the latter case he is
self-depreciating and has the aforesaid lack of
sense. Men kiss from theory and gauge a
woman's honor and womanhood by her accep-
tance or refusal; women—or girls—kiss from
impulse, trust and affection, and it means as
little to one as to the other—in entirely different ways. It means little to him, because *he*
kisses or tries to kiss any and every girl; it
signifies little to her aside from the trust and
belief that he is giving her genuine affection.
It does not mean sincerity on his part, and

even in the conceited prerogative he cannot
understand that she may give him preference.

. . . . . .

It is an awful admission to make, isn't it,
Phryne—that a man cannot trust a girl who
kisses him? Think of one's own self-respect
being so routed! He is falsely respectful to
her. He cultivates her, he entertains her, he
allows her to share his pleasures; many times
he places her in false and compromising positions, he pays her every attention, he does everything to win her affection, then if she per-
mits a kiss, he adds her to his list of girls not
to be trusted! If she refuses, then he marries
her. Why? Simply because he must have
that kiss! Think of that, Phryne! He tells
her of her glorious womanhood, of his respect
for her, of her height above other women—all
because she would not kiss him! Him!!!
You see he knows himself so well. She marries him, and she believes in his fidelity. He
is faithful and loyal while the kisses are new,
and then—divorce. Such men, Phryne, dear,
are an awfully bad lot. They make the worst
kind of husbands in a way. It is they who
finally shatter the faith of a woman. You
know, too, they have for themselves just one

religion, just one hope of heaven, just one
thing to tie to after all else palls—this " faith "
they shatter so easily.   Strange, isn't it?

.   .   .   .   .   .

Phryne, if kisses miss it—marriage—good,
honest women should not be too prudish.   It
causes a lot of sorrow.

XXII.

What do I want in love?—I am inclined to think it could not be tangibly defined with words—Well? That is it! I want love that is *not* tangible.

.   .   .   .   .   .

I have had love that is tangible; I had it with Under-the-Grass and Over-the-Grass. It was a failure. It was sharp-edged, pain-whetted, storm-tossed. It was Alps-high happiness and depths-of-the-sea despair. It was stifling with the one and suffocating with the other; and then, in the aftermath, there was nothing left but aimless drifting. It was all, when summed up, *awful*.

.   .   .   .   .   .

But this love that is not tangible? It is surviving, it is interesting. It is, though I have never confessed it, I presume it is— Jack.

.   .   .   .   .   .

Surely it is surviving, and not for one min-

ute does its interest lag. Why? My dear,
dear self, it is because it has the charm of
some doubts—the reticence, the reserve, that
suggests obstacles. Love must have difficult-
ies. To withdraw them is fatal, and even
truest love would then become a sleeping
thing. You must like, you must believe in a
man—a man in a woman—and then with something, a great deal unexpressed, love is easy,
can even become maddening.

. . . . . .

There must be companionship. Not the
companionship that can roll and light a cigarette for him and for yourself, but the kind
that gives him the easy chair and allows him
to envelop you in a cloud of fragrant smoke
while you half recline among the cushions on
the couch in a dainty tea-gown. Not the
companionship that listens to and tells *risque*
stories, but the kind that reads between the
lines, as it were, that understands and appre-
ciates the part left untold. Not the companionship that dwells upon personalities, that
narrow down to yourself and himself, but the
kind that is knowledge-fed and wit-sharpened
by being alive to the *things* which make 'up
life in a general way. In fact, my dear self,

there must be the companionship of equal intelligence, equal understanding, equal interest, equal—I was going to say equal learning,
but that would have been an error; equal
learning would be a rock to split upon.   Different experiences make different learning,
and leave something for equal intelligence
to bat up against—to keep interest alive.

.   .   .   .   .   .

This part that is not tangible?   It is something that holds you even stronger when you
are away from him than when you are with
him.   It is the something that is understood
—felt.   It tells you the thought, the consciousness in the heart irrespective of words.
You feel his glance, though you do not see
him.   Without his glance you are aware that
he is as conscious as you.   Without words
you know that he understands you.

.   .   .   .   .   .

You cannot tell just how it all came about.
You know simply that it is there, and that it
came with no effort on your part or on his—
if you could tell, then it would not be there.

.   .   .   .   .   .

This—something, this subtle something—
does not take much form, does not revolve it-

self, on your part, into any future. You are
satisfied with it as it is—for the present. You
have known so much of " form " of " future "
of the tangible, of the real, of the expressed.

.   .   .   .   .   .

Still in all reason, lying here among the pillows in this dear little retreat of a den you
know that it cannot always go on this way—
you, my dear own self and Jack. The reticence, the reserve of personalities, the diamond-cut-diamond, the sharpening of steels,
will, some day, be broken in upon. Some
day, something, perhaps some shock, will
make crystals of the glass you two are looking
through, and all the pent-up nature in both
will—no, I think not. I would not be sur-
prised if Jack and I—even if I gave him the
answer favorable to his unanswered question—
still went on with much that is unexpressed
in words. We are too worldly-wise to destroy
love's most irresistible charm. It is the intelligent undercurrent of social life that gives
zest and zeal to its surface.

.   .   .   .   .   .

Dear me, I have actually been serious. This
will never do! If Jack should chance to come
in now he could almost get that answer. As

a matter of fact, he is not worrying much about it. That "subtle something," the part that is not "tangible," tells him too much. I must return to some of my "systems."

XXIII.

"Young America—Double action"—it has no action now. It is rusty. The dear girl—or some one—has removed all the cartridges—can't move the trigger. I wonder if she hammered the thing a bit to spoil it? Surely, it can never be a "friend" again; but she need not have worried.

. . . . . .

Phryne, dear, here is something—this little revolver is something real to laugh at. It is over a year since I saw it. As I look at it now, it seems as if it could not have been I—that I never did see it—that it was only a dream. Somebody says, truly, that all things are dreams at the last, and that it is better to be dreaming than to be weeping.

. . . . . .

But, Phryne, that poor devil of a woman did not weep much. A sob catches my breath as I laugh; I actually feel a pity for that woman—that woman who was once myself! It does not seem possible that a little over a

year ago I looked upon this murderous thing
with affection, and as a swift, sure way to
peace and happiness—does it?

.   .   .   .   .   .

Just let me get a good look at you, my dear,
dear widow. . . . You are swaying, smiling, *svelte*, careless and luxurious. Ah, that is
right—you raise your hands to the back of
your blonde, fluffy head. Your chin is tilted
saucily, and there are imps in your two eyes,
but, my dear self, even your best friends cannot say that you are a beauty; you are only
effective. Blondes are never beauties. In
this tapestry-surrounded mirror, which doubles
the size of this tiny den, even your most devoted enemies would admit that you are effective. You were a poor devil of a woman
then—crushed—with this little burlesque of a
revolver seeming to be the only friend that
could help you; now, you are devilish. You
know yourself. You know that this pale-blue
clinging gown, with its laces and ribbons falling with the lines of your—your—I might
as well be honest, as I am alone—your graceful and well-trained curves, is enchanting.
You know, too, that with the cultivation of all
the senses, all the luxuries, that the heart is

resting. Why? It had to rest. It was over-
worked.

. . . . . .

You are not so bad in looks, my dear self,
but you are not so grand in womanhood as
you were when you turned to the little revolver as your friend. You appeal more to
the senses now, and you do not care a flip for
the soul—your soul or anybody's soul. You
are not wicked—for two reasons; you are indifferent, and you have pride—but souls? You
exhausted yourself on souls, a year ago or
more, in that terrible search for the soul of
Over-the-Grass. You even hunted for a soul
in that woman. Funny? I should think so!
That laugh is genuine, but, dear self, if I look
at you any longer in the mirror, I am afraid
the tears will come; I don't know why—not
for you—you are all right, but there is something about you that reminds me of the poor
devil who was so hurt a year or so ago.

. . . . . .

Hurt? So awfully hurt that the little revolver seemed the only way to get away from
the pain. Think of that, Phryne—to want to
die yourself, to get away from another's sin!
One can imagine the temptation to end it all

that comes with one's own remorse and despondency, but a heart so filled with the agony of another's wrong-doing that death seems near, and yet will not come to you unless you help it!

.   .   .   .   .   .

Isn't it tiny and pretty, with its pearl handle? It was given to me in such a beautiful way—by such a grand man—I am glad that he died before he knew of the sorrow that came to his little friend. He said:

" Put it in your pocket. In this trip you are going to take you will find that the wife, or the sister, or the sweetheart of every army officer in that Indian-infested part of the country has a revolver or a knife with which to protect her honor. She is under oath to her loved ones to take her own life before falling a victim to a red devil."

I saw red devils. My hand rested on the handle of the little thing once or twice as it nestled in my pocket, but there was no need. The Indians were considerate.

.   .   .   .   .   .

Was I a coward a year ago when I took it up, and, before the mirror, tried to find the spot I had heard discussed as bringing instant

—relief? It seemed only justice. I could not understand why I should be made to live with such suffering. *God!* It was beyond words.

.   .   .   .   .   .

But I lowered my arm and placed you on the dresser, little thing. I thought, perhaps, there were others who would mourn, who would miss me, and then dear Matie came in —saw you—took you.

.   .   .   .   .   .

Others have wondered since, my little pearl-handled toy, why I never thought of using you against that woman. That woman? It was not she who was crushing me. She was beneath me. She could not hurt me. It was Over-the-Grass. She was nothing to me. He was my husband. I think Over-the-Grass dug the heart out of me and left only bleeding, straggling, jagged shreds—a year ago.

.   .   .   .   .   .

The funniest part of it all is that *now* my laugh is so genuine. I am glad that I am alive —am living. Do you know what I am going to do with you, my pretty, rusty, useless little revolver? I am going to tie a dainty ribbon to you—glossy satin—with—a graceful—bow

—and—ends. There! Now, I am going to hang you—where shall I hang you? It really makes little difference. Here—I will add you to the collection of these national knives. Take your place, " Young America "—minus action —with these Chinese Highbinders' murderous implements and these Mexican blades.

.   .   .   .   .   .

There's quite a style about you. You do not look as if there was a thing personal about you. It would be a great shock to Jack if he could know that dainty, effeminate baby me had ever contemplated pulling your trigger with the—the—what do they call it—muzzle? —against my temple.

Ah, well, a year is a life ended and another begun. One the dream and the other the awakening.

XXIV.

My dear widow, you are certainly in deep water. Here you are caught in the trap of one of your own opinions. You are fond of saying that words and explanations count for naught, that "it is action that stands indelibly—," and, what did you do? Do? Collapsed —actually collapsed—and dropped to the floor, with Jack standing there!

.   .   .   .   .   .

I would like to ask you, my dear self, how you are going to get out of it? It is exceedingly difficult, at times, to meet emergencies when one is "on guard," but I flatter myself that I succeed admirably; off guard—, well, evidently, I am a flat. Surely, I was never more off guard—not even a jostle from my intuition to tell me that it was Over-the-Grass at the other telephone!

.   .   .   .   .   .

Meeting Jack in the hall, and saying, "I am going to the telephone," was all right, but to add "Come with me" was asinine! It is

only women with futures that can afford to
handle trifles so carelessly—not women with
"pasts." One never can tell what the "trifle"
may contain to affect the present. I thought,
of course, it was Reta or Edith, from whom I
was expecting a telephone call. To say, im
pulsively, " Come with me," to a man who is
—who is—who is Jack, is a good point in the
" system ;" it shows conclusively, even in the
unexpected, that there is nothing hidden in
your life. There really isn't anything hidden,
only I would not like to go into detail about
some things with Jack. Jack has ideas, and
some times there is pleasure in doing things—
without ideas.

.   .   .   .   .   .

Jack trifles some himself—innocent larks,
with touches of deviltry in them. These
things are just as interesting to women as to
men. Lately, since I discovered, accidentally,
that Jack escorted Evelyn to the theatre, without a party, or her husband, my nice sense of
honor to him has been somewhat dulled—I
have attended afternoon teas. Teas—and teas
where there are bright men as well as bright
women, and where the " tea," though served
in cups, is not necessarily from Japan, Ceylon,

China or Johore. Men do not like and some
women do not always like straight tea.

. . . . . .

Men, this year, are enjoying afternoon teas.
Not Jack. He abhors the thing. I have not
told him there are variations in these teas. It
would not do to demoralize him, or make him
lose faith in anything so effeminately innocent
as an "afternoon tea." It is about the only
thing left to Jack, socially, to which he can
pin his faith.

. . . . . .

When the telephone call came, I took it for
granted it was something about a "tea."
Surely, Jack could hear—just an innocent tea.
So he sauntered with me to the 'phone, in his
careless, indifferent way. I took my pose,
with the trumpet to my ear—there is really a
great opportunity at a telephone to show fetch-
ing and natural grace. Jack stood leaning
against a marble column, near the telephone
niche. He was a picture himself.

. . . . . .

I said "Hello" and heard not Reta's voice,
nor Edith's. It was a man's voice with something strangely familiar about it—something
that caused a chill to my blood—something

that stopped for an instant my pulse-beat. I forgot that Jack stood there. I only heard that voice and saw nothing. I was blinded with rushing memories and the flashing of a dead past. I said faintly: "Who is it?" and the answer came:

"I must see you. If you do not come to me, I will come to you. I hear that you are to marry——"

. . . . . .

Over-the-Grass! I did not faint. Oh, no; I only could not stand. As I fell I ejaculated his name. Jack picked me up and brought me into the den. He placed me among the cushions—and then! He stood back with folded arms and looked at me. His face was white and stern. He said finally:

"Now I understand. You have not given me my answer because—you love *him*."

I was not chilled any more. My blood was boiling. I was furious at myself. His accusation was not true, but what could I say? I had been knocked off my feet mentally and physically, but not for love of the owner of that voice which had come over the telephone wire. It was not a time for "systems," but only a system would help me. If I denied it

strenuously Jack would not believe me. He
would consider it pride on my part. I would
put the burden of the proof on him. So I said:

"Do I love him? Really, I do not think so."

"Your own theory is that acts count and
not words."

"Yes, that is true. Still it may be nerves
—it was a shock."

Jack commenced to walk up and down the
floor in his old impetuous manner. There
was no careless indifference now. He finally
wheeled and said:

"May I ask what that fellow wanted?"

Fellow! Over-the-Grass a "fellow." Gracious! How time and circumstances change
things.

"Wanted to see me."

"Where is he?"

"I don't know—my knees gave out."

"I will find out."

.   .   .   .   .   .

And off went my polished, reserved, man-
of-the-world Jack. I haven't seen him since,
and that was—only a few hours ago, but it
seems ages.

There is one great comfort; I am all right
now, and ready to laugh again.

XXV.

Phryne, I am restless.   This dainty den is
full of shadows.   The shadows that I liked
for their atmosphere of peace and seclusion
are now seemingly filled with menace—of
some coming evil that I cannot ward away.
Even you, in your marble silence, suggest
something that will only bring unrest.   Bacchante, there, in her bronze and unconscious
pose, joyful and out of the pale of all worldliness, seems a burden to me.   It seems as if
she, too, needed protection—protection where
there is no protection.

.   .   .   .   .   .

What is it, Phryne?   Why are we never
able to get away from what has once filled our
lives, our hearts?

.   .   .   .   .   .

The days have been long, the nights longer
since that telephone message from Over-the-
Grass.   Why?   I don't know.   It is simply
unrest.

.   .   .   .   .   .

If one could only make of these sorrows

graves in the earth, instead of in the heart!
That is not original, Phryne. Tom, in his
lovely, tender, Irish way of looking at things,
said that one day, and it struck home. I have
thought of it so many times. A grave in the
earth does not open. If it did, and the dear
dead could come back to us, happiness
only would accompany them. These graves
in the heart, when they open, give to us again
the sorrows that we would so gladly put away.

.   .   .   .   .   .

Phryne, dear, we can pretend to laugh, and
we can laugh in the calm that settles down
into our lives after the terrific storm, but the
laugh, or rather the smile, is only the other
name for a tear. Pathos and humor trot along
so closely side by side that as the laughter in
the voice ripples it is caught in the reef of a
sob; as the tear fills the eye a smile on the
lips can meet it and absorb it. One is as sad
at times as the other.

.   .   .   .   .   .

There are times in the dark of the night,
Phryne—let me whisper it to you—I would
not have anyone to know—that I can hear a
voice that has passed out of my life calling
me—calling me with tense tones of yearning.

I start up and I step out of the bed to go before I am quite awake and before I know that it is only a dream.

. . . . . .

For months, Phryne, that voice has called me at night, and though I smile through the day the—the dream has made me tired—has made me restless. I am not myself and I feel that I am so weak that even pride would be gone if again I should see—the owner of the voice.

. . . . . .

Phryne, if what we call society were only better—if it condemned in men what it condemns in women—wives would be better protected and there would not be so many rent homes, hearts and lives. Men would not so dare to trifle; wives would not spend two-thirds of their days forgiving that which makes their own lives so sad that there are times when the long sleep seems preferable to all that could be so beautiful if—   That if !

. . . . . .

"If " is a word that holds so much and so little. It is just the feverish pleasure that comes with the few hours, or days, or even months, when conscience sleeps and the sense

of honor is gone. Then there is the awakening to a lifelong regret, the shame—unless,
perchance, society has had an opportunity to
close its eyes, and has not seen too much.   If
there is a loophole for doubt it ignores the
sin and fawns upon the sinner.   It basks in
the danger to itself.   It feels the pleasure
there is in balancing on the edge of a precipice and not falling over—smiling always at
the sinner if he be a man, and drawing its
skirts away from the woman who shared his
sin.   Phryne, men with "reputations" are
fascinating, in society, if the reputation is
gilded with only gossip.   Of course, a scandal
that is public is different.   Society would not
countenance that—oh, dear, no!

. . . . . .

Reputations can be gilded again, but there
is one thing that will not take the gold-leaf,
and that is love.   If faith and trust are
knocked out of it you can pile into the jagged
edges a sympathy; but love can never again
be what it was.   Sympathy and pity never
take the place of faith.

. . . . . .

I seem to be arguing with myself on a serious subject—eh, Phryne?   No, not exactly.

I am arguing—there is no argument. I am
only looking into the grave in the heart that
has been opened by that telephone call. Jack
is silent about it. I wondered what I would
say to the dear fellow—what explanation I
would make for being knocked off my feet at
the sound of a voice. When he said, " You
love *him*," it certainly looked bad for explanations. But Jack is always wise. He is cool
and he is cautious. He would never fight
against the inevitable. He would understand,
too, perfectly, after the first instant, just as
well as I. Afterward he said only, " You must
not see Over-the-Grass." He did not say it so
severely as sadly—not for himself, but for me.

. . . . . .

But, Phryne, I think I would like to see
Over-the-Grass once more. I want to look at
him, and to study him with the knowledge
and full realization that all those protesta-
tions to me of love and loyalty were false,
and that another woman at the same time was
hearing the same words.

. . . . . .

I want to see him once more, and then I
can forget him. I will know then that the
voice I hear in the night is really only a dream.

XXVI.

Ah, my conscious marble Phryne and my
unconscious bronze Bacchante, I am in disgrace.   It looks as if I would never get out
of the deep water into which I plunged
when I collapsed at the sound of a voice
over the telephone — the voice of Over-
the-Grass.   It could all have been managed
better if Jack had not been standing there.   He
cannot understand why the unexpected voice
should have overpowered me unless love for its
owner is still lying dormant in my heart.   It
is probably the blindness of jealousy on Jack's
part.   He ought to know that there are other
things just as strong as love in a woman's
heart.

.   .   .   .   .   .

I dropped to the floor at the sound of the
voice because of the shock.   I am not responsible for that.   This floundering still in
" deep water " is because since then I have
been too honest.   It is very wrong.   One must
not be honest with anyone but one's self.

.   .   .   .   .   .

I did not realize that cool, debonair, careless Jack was capable of excitement in his love for me. Once or twice I have seen his hands tremble and fire flash in his eyes, but he has been so seemingly indifferent about my delayed answer, and though he has at times asserted himself in a way that showed no doubt in his mind about my marrying him eventually, he has appeared satisfied to drift along. He seemed to be waiting patiently until I should know myself as well as he knew me. Of course, I had no hesitancy in saying to him that I wanted to see Over-the-Grass once more. It was true—why not say it to Jack?

   .   .   .   .   .   .

I did not go into detail about it. I was not so very sure myself why I had—have this desire. Only one thing is sure—it is *not* love. I want to look into the eye of Over-the Grass with all my faith crushed by my knowledge of truths. I want to see how those eyes will look when the lips *cannot* tell me all that is false. I remember how truthful they looked, to me, with the lies—how will they look when he is compelled to tell me horrible truths?

   .   .   .   .   .   .

I did not tell Jack all these things. I did

not tell him that always, in the days when
Over-the-Grass was not—when I was not the
widow that is not a widow—this false faith
that is in the heart of a woman made me believe, because I must believe. How else could
I, in my pride, live my life? Women believe
because they must believe. They forgive, and
it is not because sense and judgment have given
no warning that faith is misplaced. It is the
way with women. Then, too, sometimes your
trust is the wrong-doer's conscience—in the
hours of remorse. If you do not believe, and
the wrong-doer knows it, then what are you?
Simply—wife or no wife — just one of the
others.

I did not tell Jack that I want to meet Over-
the-Grass when he cannot say, " I swear to you
by the grave of my dead mother that I am,
literally, true to you." You see, Phryne, I
really did believe him when he said that!

.   .   .   .   .   .

I want to see if even now he has the strength
of his wickedness and can speak honestly of
his treachery to me and to his own manhood.
I want to look at the man who for several
years built up his manhood, with me, on my
faith and trust in him and represented himself

as something that he was not. I want to hear
what he will say when he cannot say, "I have
been true to you." You see, Phryne, I was
so dreadfully deceived. I want to see if his
face looks the same with truths as with those
awful untruths. Just curiosity, Phryne.

.   .   .   .   .

I only said to Jack :
" I want to see him once more."

.   .   .   .   .   .

Jack ? Jack stood up. His face was white.
His eyes were a reflection of so much that I
have not seen in him before. At first he spoke
slowly :
" You are, after all—a woman. You are all
alike. You, my queen, my ideal, my reality—
you, even you, are like the rest. You, my
proud one, can take, figuratively, beatings,
bruises ; can let him drag you by the hair of
the head, tear out your heart, crush your pride,
your life, insult you privately, openly, and
still—cling to him !

.   .   .   .   .   .

" *Him !* A man who knew no honor toward
wife or friends ; who insulted you as woman
was never before insulted ; who allowed you
to breathe the same air as the vile specimen for

whom at the last he sacrificed everything;
who allowed you, his own wife, to plead with
her not to ruin his life; who allowed you to
be placed on the defensive between himself
and her, telling you in her presence—the
woman with whom he had been disgracing
himself for six weeks—that you were making
a mistake, were making a scene, that this
woman was only a patient of his; who allowed—in the hours that you plead and tried
to save him from the disgrace that you felt intuitively was coming—allowed this vile thing,
who is a blot even on the *demi-monde*, allowed
her to laugh at you! *Laugh*—think of it!—
while you were asking only for your own husband, your life, his life—this thing that was
dragging him to the depths of depravity—to
laugh at *you*. And you want to see him!
This man who was once your husband, whom
you shielded always, because of his high pro-
fession; this man who at the last was so blinded
by infatuation that he could not see the chance
he had, that you gave to him, even then, to
save himself. *This* is the man you want to
see once more! My God!—am *I* nothing to
you?"

Phryne, there was something I discovered then that I never felt before. I can't tell you. But Jack, grand, glorious, passionate Jack, was so much to me that I could only look at him—speechless. I was afraid, too, Phryne—afraid of something, I know not what, but I could not tell him. I think if I had, if I *could* have told him how much he was to me, that he would have taken me in his arms, and I would have—died. My heart stifles me sometimes.

.   .   .   .   .   .

I only looked at him. I must have looked coldly. I was cold. My lips were frozen.

.   .   .   .   .   .

Jack came to me and knelt at my side. He said :

" My soul is yours. I have placed you so high, so sacred, that, while you are all that appeals to a man's most sensuous nature, I would not touch your hand until you voluntarily gave me the right. I have waited for your answer. Sometime you *will* be my wife. Can you not see that my soul is on fire for you ? That my manhood to me can never reach the height where I can feel myself worthy of you ? And yet you, my queen, my pet, can

want to see this man? Is it true—*do* you want
to see him?"

.   .   .   .   .   .

And my lips said—" Yes."

.   .   .   .   .   .

Phryne—my heart is light—never so light
—it must be love! Love for Jack.   Yet—I
must see Over-the-Grass—once.

.   .   .   .   .   .

When I said " yes " Jack kissed my hair
and went away.   He will come back.

XXVII.

Do I know myself? Yes. Perhaps toc well.

.   .   .   .   .   .

Phryne, before you were immortalized into marble, physical perfection, I do not suppose that you, in life, ever knew an unrest. You had your beautiful self! Your beauty had adulation. You were satisfied. To have an unrest come into your life that you cannot thrust away is, I think sometimes, worse than all other sorrows—the unrest that is forced upon you, the something for which you were not prepared, and which, in its being unexpected, bars all philosophy. It leaves you stranded, in a way, with the foundation knocked from under life's plans.

.   .   .   .   .   .

I do not know just how to tell it, how to express it—but I think that, if I *must* suffer, and I realized it could not be averted, if I could but know even a few minutes before it comes, then I would be resigned. If one I loved should die I would want him to know

that he was going to take the last sleep, and
that he be willing for it to come. If I should
die—dying is nothing, if one only knows. If
one cannot know what is coming to us in sorrow, then there is left in the trail of it the
unrest—a something not complete—even sorrow itself. If we *know*, we can finish.

I am vague, Phryne—as vague as unrest.
I do not know how to put it into words, but I
have had unrest ; that which comes from sudden death, and again that from sudden sorrow.

And so, Phryne, when I said "yes" after
Jack's grand, honest and manly pleading, and
felt that I still wanted to see Over-the-Grass
once, I was not foolish, wicked or selfish. I
wanted to get rid of the unrest that has en-
veloped me of late. It is a terrible thing to
be left stranded mentally. If it were financially, it would not be so bad. One could
work and forget. To have the greatest part
of your life drop out like a flash, you, at least,
afterward want something that will prove to
you tangibly that all is as it should be, and
that you do not want it again. If I had felt
that I could not see Over-the-Grass again it

would have been because of one of two
reasons; the mixture of love and hate, or the
fear of his power over me. I had neither of
these reasons. I wanted an opportunity to
resign myself voluntarily to the inevitable.

.   .   .   .   .   .

After the plain and humiliating truths told
me by Jack, after knowing the probable risk
I ran in losing his highest regard, I still said
I must see Over-the-Grass once. And dear
Jack! When he sadly and disappointedly
kissed my hair and went away—*he arranged
it.* What a man is Jack! Where is another
who could be so generous? Jack believes in
taking people as they are and not for what he
wants them to be. He knew if I still said
" yes " it was because it was true and because
I would not deceive him. It might disap-
point him in me, it might be different from
what he himself would do, but he is too much
of a philosopher to want to make me over, to
mould me or to change me. If that inner
most soul of mine could not be what he would
like, then—well, at least, he would know me
as I am. A little later he will know it was
better; just now Jack's best judgment is
clouded because in his heart he feels that I

would not have seen Over-the-Grass if he himself were all to me that he would be. Who
but Jack would have brought him to me?

Was it design that he suggested my seeing
Over-the-Grass here in my den? It was a
great stroke. Over-the-Grass is not—was not
built for "dens." This den, Phryne and Bacchante—ah, poor Bacchante!—if your bronze
ears could hear all this worldliness, this modern
life that has been about you of late!—this den,
these draperies, this statuary, these paintings,
the fireplace, the twilights, the reveries, the
peaceful, quiet luxury, the lounging laziness,
have developed since Over-the-Grass went out
of my life. He is not, never could be, a part
of it.

.   .   .   .

As he came into the niche, where I live
some part of each day, I knew instantly that
I had grown away from him. It was a glaring,
instantaneous fact. I knew at once that my
"unrest" had been *rest*. I had been blind.
The unrest was Over-the-Grass himself—*himself*. His very presence, his great personal
magnetism, is a storm of the soul, not the
peace of it. He gives no rest—no silent contentment. The after-dinner coffee, the cigar.

the sweet after-dinner hours that I have known
with Jack, I could never know with Over-the-
Grass. He could not sit down in the luxury
and quiet of idleness for an hour—with me.
He could not realize that communion that is
expressed without words. If he had an hour
of his own, it would be " pool," billiards, a
ride, a drive, a flirtation, a sensation—always
a sensation. Over-the-Grass is up or down
—stimulated hilarity or the despair of remorse. He could not come into the dainty
den and forget himself in the luxury
of it.

> .   .   .   .   .   .

No one will ever know, Phryne, how my
heart acted when I knew that he was coming.
It thumped, jumped, stopped, started again.
Once before I had seen him for an instant. It
was unexpected, and I met it coolly and with
indignation. My heart was untouched. It
was different now. There were things to be
said, a balance to be struck, a future to be decided. My idol—no, my pride—had been
shattered. My husband was gone, the man
coming—who had once been he—had belonged for weeks to another woman. I was
to look at him, and for once I was to hear

truths from him, and know, too, that with it all he still loved me. And I?

. . . . . .

My heart was quiet again as he came in. I don't want to think of that hour, Phryne. It was sad. It could be nothing else. It was so sad that the unrest is all gone. I am satisfied. I know now why men cannot tell their wives truths about their peccadillos. It is because of the deep respect to the women who bear their names. Phryne, the lie is a compliment to the wife's womanhood. Men can tell horrible truths to the women who are the companions of debaucheries, but not to the women whom they respect.

. . . . . .

I had thought at the last to hear all the truth from Over-the-Grass and it would help me to forget. But he could not tell me. I did not want it, after all. He said that I belonged to him, that I was his in God's sight, that I must not marry, that it would be sacrilege, that the decree of the court was not right, that I was still his wife.

. . . . . .

I did not argue; I did not contradict. I listened. I saw that his hair had whitened at the temples. I saw that he had suffered. There were lines of anguish in his face. The proud shoulders were a bit stooped. I saw that nature had intended him, more than most men, for a magnificent man. I realized that women can be vultures and that men can be their victims, just as much as women can be tools to masculine deviltry. I knew and felt that he was right, that I did belong to him, but—I could not go back into the shadows. I had no faith to sustain me. A woman needs blind faith to make life endurable with men like Over-the-Grass.

. . . . . .

I cannot think about it. My unrest is gone. I am satisfied. I want to see Jack very much. I wonder why he does not come?

XXVIII.

Phryne! I think that it is censure that makes nuns of women—worldly women.

. . . . . .

That tabby aunt of mine has actually brought blushes—horrible, uncomfortable blushes—to my cheeks. I do not know that I want to be a nun, but I do feel—upset. My dear, my dainty, dreamy, beautiful den is, evidently, no place for Aunt Tabby.

. . . . . .

When you come to think of it, Phryne, now that we are brought up standing, as it were, it must have been a great shock to that country aunt of mine. I had forgotten a lot of things and people that still exist. I had thought to give her pleasure when I sent for her to come right up to my sanctum. I gave her—well, there were two of us; I gave her and she gave me.

. . . . . .

Our sins were multiplied. I was in evening dress—not so *very*, but "housey," and you, Phryne and Bacchante, are, in your marble

and in your bronze, as the sculptor created
you. She said she blushed as much for me as
for you. At first I did not realize, then, as
she went on, I blushed, too, those horrible
burning blushes—I blush again to think of it.
I blushed, not for you, Phryne and Bacchante,
nor for myself, but for the horrible depths of
lewdness to which a feminine mind can dive.

.   .   .   .   .   .

There are some women that cannot be edu-
cated. I wonder if I know a man who could
have so embarrassed me? She said that I was
immodest through cultivation, and that she
was thankful that she was ignorant and mod-
est. Aunt Tabby is not an ignorant woman.
As she talked on, there were times when she
was quite eloquent. She said that all sense of
modesty had long ago disappeared in cities;
that with the nude in art—paintings and statuary—the ballet, the burlesque, the demand
for realism in novels and on the stage, the
meaning of the word modesty had been forgotten. What made me blush furiously was
when she turned her back to you, Phryne and
Bacchante, and—to me, so that her eyes would
not be polluted by the sight of us. Rather
funny—eh, Phryne?

.   .   .   .   .   .

Poor Aunt Tabby ! She cannot understand
that the modesty that accompanies ignorance
is a misnomer ; that the mind can be purified
and the lewdness weeded out of it through a
higher cultivation.   She cannot discover, now,
the dainty divinity of nature in your translucent curves, Phryne.   She cannot see that the
sculptor in his creations has discovered something better and purer in the outline of the
human form than has been known to her. She
will not understand that the sculptor has tried
to teach us purity by taking away from his
production that which appeals only to the
coarser element in humanity.   She could not
understand the story told of beauty, love and
trouble in your bowed head, Phryne, nor could
she see the innocence, the unconsciousness, the
purity of both mother and child in your pose,
Bacchante.   She saw simply—naked women.
She honestly thought to establish her own
goodness with me by the position that she
took.   I believe that she was honestly shocked.

.   .   .   .   .   .

And I thought to give Aunt Tabby pleasure !
When I brought her into the nook I thought
to see her drop into the easy-chair with a sigh
of contentment.   What could be more ex-

quisite than it is to-night, with the glow of
the lamps through the colored shades, the
grayish warm blue of the walls, the soft tints
of draperies and cushions? It seemed to me
I was giving her a glimpse of heaven. She
saw only us—it was to her not heaven!

.   .   .   .   .   .

To me it was sacrilege to my den. One
thing is perfectly apparent: Aunt Tabby may
be honest, but she is fully aware of the im-
purity—to her—of the human outlines. She
cannot be taught *anything* that will deepen
her blushes. If she would but study a bit the
" cultivated immodesty " which she now condemns it would have but one effect and could
do her no harm. She would learn from the
sculptor and the artist from what standpoint
and knowledge of humanity the purity of expression in art creation is derived. The
sculptor and artist do not try to improve
upon nature; neither do they ask the public
to worship and applaud in their productions
what is condemned in nature. They themselves, in their higher intelligence, give to us
the pristine purity before human minds became
draped with ignoble thoughts.

.   .   .   .   .   .

Phryne and Bacchante, I shall not drape
you, but when Aunt Tabby comes again—if
she ever does—I will receive her in the draw-
ing-room and I will wear a high-necked dress.

XXIX.

Over-the-Grass *saying* things ! Well ! Well !

.   .   .   .   .   .

When he thought I would forgive, he ex-
alted me.   When he knows that I cannot love
him again he—says things.

.   .   .   .   .   .

Really, my dear cold, marble Phryne, that
ought to suffuse your statuesque curves with a
red glow.

.   .   .   .   .   .

It is strange, but a perfectly natural trait of
character in those—men or women—who are
capable of dishonorable acts.

.   .   .   .   .   .

I think it is time for me to laugh again.
I really thought that Over-the-Grass—women
are so gullible !   It did really seem to me that
Over-the-Grass honored me so, even in his own
dishonor, that I was perfectly safe against this
customary viciousness of the wrong-doer.   I
cannot help smiling at my gullibility.   Surely
I must be bullet-proof against ordinary common sense.   Lalla says I have changed of late.

It was true. I had been taking things seriously, and had forgotten my lesson—had actually forgotten to smile at all these trifles. I
was seeing reality—heart instead of head,
goodness instead of badness, sadness instead
of selfishness in—events. I had for several
weeks *felt* and *thought.* I expect it was a reaction. I had been smiling indiscriminately,
for some time, at all that terrible suffering.
Lately, though, the smile was against myself;
it seemed a bit cruel. I actually thought
Over-the-Grass was suffering because he had
lost me. It saddened me. I knew so well
what it all meant.

.   .   .   .   .   .

You don't know, Phryne. I ought not to
think about it, but—well, your husband kisses
you tenderly and says, "Good-bye, sweetheart, I will be home in an hour." He goes
out leaving you glad that you are alive, and
that clouds that looked dark are disappearing.
You are aglow again with a happy love and
trust. One hour ticks away into the second
one. You do not mind. You have him to
think about. You are willing to wait because
waiting is dreaming, and you know that your
dream is real. The second hour passes into

the third one. The happy love and trust is
chilling a bit. Midnight! It seems a long
time back to the after-dinner good-bye. Your
lip trembles a little.

. . . . . .

Then the telephone rings. You are told
that the husband may not come home to-night.
The reason given is a good one, but a moan
comes from your heart. Down there in the
heart depths you always realize the shaky
foundation on which your trust is built. He
does not "come home to-night," nor the
next. You wait, wait—your heart chilling in
stony, silent misery.

. . . . . .

The nights and days of waiting are not all
your own. Others want him, need him.
Then you learn the sacredness, the holiness of
well-told lies. You do not know until then
that lies can appear to you God-given. But
you must protect his good name. You know
now what "for better, for worse" means.
It is the very worst, because faithful James,
as he sees your suffering and your patience,
tells you that he went out for a last good-bye
with "that woman." It is all the more
necessary that the good name be protected.

Something must be saved. So you lie to this
one and that one. You give him a chance to
save himself. He will not have it.

. . . . . .

Weeks come and then months. The good-
bye for an hour must have meant good-bye
for all time, and yet there had been no prepar-
ation. Is it the publicity or the infatuation
that is keeping him away? Then comes a
missive to you from a stranger written from
Oklahoma, another afterward from Dakota.
This missive from a kind stranger tells you of
this woman, assumed names, disguise. What
does it mean? Just one thing to you—the
end. You must now think of yourself.

. . . . . .

You have defended him. You have given
him his chance. In thinking of yourself, you
take the smallest of his crimes against you—
the one that will disgrace him the least—you
cannot forget what he has been to you—and
the court grants you freedom instantly. You
turn down this leaf in your life, and then
learn to smile at the irony of fate and the
credulity of women.

. . . . . .

He comes back. He tells you frankly of

his "escapade," of his being the victim of circumstances, of his love for you, which holds him through all that dissipation. You do not forgive him, but you pity him. It is not the contemptuous pity that others give him. It is genuine: it seems a horror that this man who stood so high could fall so low ; that this man who has such a knowledge of morality could himself be such a moral monstrosity. You do what you can for him, and you ask others to be kind to him.

. . . . . .

Then you leave him the field. You come away. It is his to find again the manhood he has lost. To the outside world he fell from the top of the cliff to the bottom suddenly, but you know that artificial props had been holding him at the top for some time. He tells you that in a year, if he can redeem himself, he will ask you to be his wife again. In a month you know the year must be commenced again ; that repentance was short-lived and used only as a straw to a drowning man.

. . . . . .

Repentance had not brought him the commendation he thought that he merited. He felt that it took bravery to come back and say that he was sorry; that few men could do it. He knew no difference between moral courage and the courage of despair.

.   .   .   .   .   .

You come away and learn to smile at the suffering that is gone, and you are happy because you are not *miserable*. Sweet dreams of long sleep, tempting revolvers, heartaches, reaching your arms to heaven for comfort in the dark of the night, waiting, waiting for something that never came—all become merely a jest to you.

.   .   .   .   .   .

Then comes once more a voice—over the telephone—that was so much to you. It brings you unrest. You smile no more here in the den all by yourself. The den seems full of shadows of coming evil. He comes to you. Your vision is clear and you see again a moral wreck. There may be a future for him, but it is not with you. The sadness of it all, weighs upon you. Lalla, Jack and others see the change.

.   .   .   .   .   .

Now, Phryne, you hear he has been saying things. It is not so sad, after all, is it? We will laugh again in the good old way here by ourselves. There is one thing, however, I would like to know. Why do men and women, when they walk into pit-holes of im- morality, try to pull others into them? Do they think, in defaming others, it lessens their own sin? If I should resent a libel of Over- the-Grass and do legally as did my friend, would he, too, beg for mercy and say that all he asks is peace? I suppose so.

.   .   .   .   .   .

Phryne, dear, the men and women who can stoop to dishonor are such cringing cowards! They will even ask for mercy from those whom they injure most. Strange, isn't it?

XXX.

Sometimes I think—no, it cannot be possible—Jack is not a man of weakness. Yet it has dawned upon me, or there has been the flicker of a dawn once or twice, that Jack has been jealous of Ned. Ned!

.   .   .   .

Let me think it over. Jack is thirty-seven. Ned is nineteen, or twenty, or twenty-one or two—I wonder just how old or how young he is? Boys such as he are as averse to telling their ages as are—some women. Anyhow, Jack is a man of the world. Ned is a boy— of the world.

.   .   .   .

Yes, surely Ned is of the world. He thinks he is " *blasé*." *Blasé !* A boy like that! He is only tired. He is tired of the world as he knows it—not of the world as it really is.

.   .   .   .

I have no doubt that this handsome boy is living the pace that *can* kill, or would bring some kind of a death to other boys at his age. Ned, however, is well balanced. He has mental

backbone. He will never be the victim of
girls or women. He is considering himself
blasé just in time to be saved. Sometime he
will love somebody sincerely and loyally, and
I suspect he has already had a lesson of the
heart in some form. It must have been a
cruel disappointment of some kind that has
taught him scepticism, and has given him
rather a full knowledge of life up to his age.
He is too young to have learned from observation, and, too, with girls, with women and
with his fellow chums, he seems to be protected by a barrier of personal reserve that is
beyond his years. His fun, his wit, his conversation, are always general, and yet, how he
can blush ! It is that which proves him alive
and not *blasé*.

   .   .   .   .   .   .

    Jack is alive, but only under the surface.
He could not blush, because he has such perfect mastery over himself. Ned is alive on
the surface, ready always to be ignited by a
new sensation. Jack would have difficulty in
finding a new sensation. I am sure that years
ago he ran the whole gamut of sensation.
There is no new sensation for Jack, unless—
it is Ned himself.

   .   .   .   .   .   .

Why has the thought come to me that Jack
could be jealous of Ned? Dear old Jack!
He is not, could not be jealous in the ordinary
sense, and jealous is not the right word to use,
but that sigh of his when he said " the laughter of youth is the soul of it," spoke volumes.
When he added : "You ought to be careful
about that boy—you are fascinating to him,"
I really think his only thought was to protect
Ned.

.   .   .   .   .   .

I ignored the last clause and said :
   " Do you mean that Ned's soul is shallow
because he can laugh so heartily ? "
   " Oh, no, child," said Jack, " but one who
can laugh so honestly feels honestly and is
capable of intense suffering."

.   .   .   .   .   .

What made me use the word jealous is
probably that Jack is a bit blind where I am
concerned. I am not fascinating to Ned in
the way Jack means. Ned likes me because
I appreciate him. Old boys and young boys
appreciate appreciation. I could not fascinate
Ned because I *would* not. I like his fun, his
pessimisms, his spontaneity, his brilliancy, his
jolly companionship. In the jollity of youth

there is a letting down of the tensions for a
woman that is impossible with an older man.
Why ? A youth does not presume. He takes
the abandon as it is; an older man takes it as
he *thinks* it is. The young man has more
faith in you and would not presume; the older
man, if there is a jolly abandon about you,
would be apt to attempt a test. But to " fascinate "—for a woman of the world, a woman
who has passed her early youth, a woman with
a " past," and a future, too—to fascinate a
youth with his future all before him, she
must herself be interested in another way.

. . . . . .

What is this fascination that exists so often
between women who have passed the earliest
youth and the young men who are in the flush
of it? First and foremost, I expect, it is a
lot of human nature in both. On the woman's
side, in the years lying back of her, and possibly also in the present, she is herself in the
power of men. She has been taught what
men have chosen to teach her. It has not
altogether satisfied her. Her teachers have
taught her entirely from their standpoint and
not from hers. So few men really understand all there is in a woman's nature. And

she, possibly, has not dared to lay bare the dissatisfaction. There is every reason why she should not if she is wise. The man who has been her teacher would not be flattered if he should discover that his own teachings have developed a knowledge greater than his own. When the vanity of a man is wounded it is death to the happiness of the two. So she learns to suppress much, a great deal that perhaps the man from whom she conceals her inner self will seek in other women.

.   .   .   .   .   .

Then, in the zenith of her womanhood, she meets the younger worldling, who is *blasé* because girls are insipid. He is attracted to her through her mentality, and without doubt her physical magnetism. She dares to be herself, and having knowledge of herself and of men, she develops his admiration up to her own standpoint. She teaches him women as she knows them herself. She plays with the edged tools of all daring because she feels that she is the stronger of the two, and that *he* will dare no further than she wills. She is charmed with the freedom she allows herself ; he is flattered by her finding in him anything that will interest a woman of her attainments and popularity. He becomes thoroughly interested, madly infatuated, and they are very rare instances where he is honestly and enduringly in love.

. . . . . .

She? Sometimes his honest devotion and adoration satisfies her to the extent that she makes the mistake, for herself, of marrying him; sometimes she sacrifices his love to her ambitions and bestows upon him the good deed (in the end) of not marrying him. If she marries him he will grow weary, because he will be with her, where she was with others before teaching was reversed. As he learns the world as it is, he will want, with women, to guide and not follow. If she, for his "own good," sacrifices his love and marries someone else, he will always remember her as an ideal woman of whom cruel Fate robbed him, and will never know that she played with him, and deliberately "fascinated" him. For it is always the woman who is first interested and wields the power over the very young man.

XXXI.

I don't care anything about the jealousies of men, but the jealousies of women make me afraid. The jealousies of men are easily taken care of—they are jealous because they love you. Women are jealous because—they don't love you.

. . . . . .

Phryne, dear, I believe that I do not like women.

. . . . . .

That is a very bad and a very asinine remark to make. If your ears were flesh and blood, instead of pure cold marble, I would not say it to you. It is decidedly idiotic for a woman to say that she does not like women, yet did you ever notice how often women say that to men? Think of a bright woman making that remark to a man who *does* like women! She says it, too, with a sparkle in her eye, and an air of expected approval. She says it as if she were perfectly sure a man would admire her for it. Does she feel that the dear sex is naturally on the defensive, and that in the declaration she proves that she has discovered and proportionately scorns all the foibles of the feminine race? Or does she think that her personal disapproval of her sex will make that man condemn all women but herself?

.   .   .   .   .   .

It is not a nice remark, Phryne, and it is most unwise, but to you, here in the seclusion of the den, it does not matter. I really think I do not like them—collectively. Individually is an entirely different matter. There are several reasons for it, Phryne. One is that at first, and sometimes all the time, women do not like me.

.   .   .   .   .   .

What was that remark of Aunt Tabby's when I once said that I thought that women did not like me as well as men did? She looked at me over her glasses and said quietly : " Well, my dear child, I am very sure that if you made yourself as agreeable in some small way to women as you do to men, they would like you just as well."

.   .   .   .   .   .

That may be so, Phryne, but men never misunderstand me and women do. Men believe that I am frank and honest and women are ready

to believe that I am not.   Men believe that I
have character, tempered with honor.   Women
know that I have plenty of individuality, but
women don't know much about honor.   They
are too—but that is another part of it.

. . . . . .

Personally, I enjoy the society of men more
because they know the world practically.
Women have theories.   Theories are tiresome in the long run.   Women are never perfectly honest with each other and seldom with
themselves.   They have preconceived ideas of
the proper things to say and do, and they try
to cram it down your throat, and will give you
no credit for having sense or intelligence to
see through the sham.   And, Phryne, there is
nothing I *hate* so much as to have women think
they are deceiving me.   I don't care what a
woman does so much if she only knows that I
am not believing that black is white.   The
contrary is a great humiliation.   As most
women do think me incapable of seeing
through a sham, I am with them in a constant
state of humiliation—so I like men better.
The shams of men, too, are so much more
quickly discovered.

Though a woman is jealous of you because she does not love you, she can love you to distraction if it is for her interest to do so. She will love you until she is interested in the man whom you love or for whom you care. Then —um-m!

.   .   .   .   .   .

Men are so blind. Now, there's Dick. He is really and truly fond of dear little Reta. I would not have believed that he could be swayed out of devoted loyalty even for a few days. It is as Jack says:

" In these modern days in metropolitan life a man follows mostly the pace a woman sets."

Gertie set the pace in her quiet, proper, mountainous way, and Dick certainly has been trotting it. Strange how a man will jump to extremes! Reta, dark, beautiful, dainty, exquisite, *petite* and sweet in her nature; Gertie, blonde, large, heavy, coarse-looking, with eyes of that indescribable gray which are for the most time half-closed, as if afraid to let you see the real self; always shocked at the slightest abandon of manner and yet always ready for wine, whisky or cocktails with this one or that one. She set the pace—which is the undercurrent, her innerself—a trait of character that will sacrifice her best friend—for what? To satisfy for a few weeks her vanity, her love of luxuries and her selfishness.

.   .   .   .   .

Men so seldom understand the inner nature, the designing nature of women. These women are unscrupulous in their dealings with both men and women. New York is full of them. They seem to be living for what they can get out of their acquaintances, instead of for what they can do for them. They will take a woman's friend, or even husband, from her by means fair or foul, and then the friendship they give to the man, for whose favor they have struggled, is based entirely on what he can do for them. They want not one friend but a dozen or more. They give as much love to all as to one, unless one should happen to be in a position to do more for them. Then the one will get the largest quantity of attention, while the others are kept dangling on the string to fill in with. The "others" would be sacrificed instantly if perchance they should interfere at all with the favored one.

.   .   .   .   .   .

They are shrewd, too, Phryne—these women. Metropolitan life teaches them the art of con-

servatism They have it down to a science.
With the innocent face, and manners of an
artless child, they learn never to let the left
hand know what the right hand is doing,
Number one, two, three, and the rest of them
can go along for months or until the play is
over, and never know of each other. The
world is so large, in a city, and can hold so
many circles. One circle is not apt to break
into another, with a little adroit managing.
These women will take your friend from you,
but if you turn about, and take a friend of
theirs—I was going to say "Wow!" Phryne.
I won't say wow, but it's cats and dogs just
the same.

.   .   .   .   .   .

A man never gives the woman with whom
he is closely associated the credit for being designing. He will accuse the sex in general of
duplicity, but the woman he knows—oh, no.
Not unless he discovers, as his interest palls,
treachery. He is in the newness of the friendship, or the "pace" she is setting, as wax in
her hands. She will intuitively understand
the kind of woman he prefers, and will be that
woman. He will learn to believe in her, and
will never understand her arts unless his eyes

are opened by another of her kind. Even if
he should know that a woman is setting the
pace for him, his vanity is flattered, and he
trots along to see what the end will be. She,
in her shrewdness, handles him with light ribbons, and he gets pleasure, with no thought of
disloyalty to the honest woman whom he is
wounding.

.   .   .   .   .   .

Phryne, it is a conviction of mine that a
woman cannot be a true friend to a woman
under *all* circumstances. I am not thinking
of Adelaide, Reta, Lalla, Ella, Matie, and several others—but even they would not love me
if I took from them—would I love either one
of them if they took from me Jack?

.   .   .   .   .   .

If Jack could be taken, I would not want
him.

XXXII.

My thoughts lately seem to be running riot
on the subject of women. I might as well
have it out with myself and get done with it.

.   .   .   .   .   .

Over-the-Grass and Under-the-Grass always
said, and so also has dear, non-committal Jack,
that I really know so little about women.
Over-the-Grass used to put it emphatically.
Once when he said, " Dearie, you are such an
idiot about women," he did not say plain idiot.
He trimmed it up. He used the word that is
expressed in writing with a dash, and which
also is the name of a small East Indian coin.
I did not mind his emphasis. While it expressed doubtful knowledge on his part, it was
in a way a compliment to me. It meant that
I thought them much better than they were. I
know more now about women. Since I have a
" past " or two of my own I have cultivated
them and studied them more.

.   .   .   .   .   .

I have to stop to smile at that word " past."
I will never hear it or say it again without

thinking of what Tom, in his funny Irish way,
said yesterday : " It is getting to be really indecent to go around without a past."

.   .   .   .   .   .

There's more or less logic in Tom's remark.
It may not be exactly indecent, but social
pasts are getting so thick that men or women
without pasts have difficulty in finding for
themselves pleasant niches.   Minus a past
and finding that to call a human being *divorcée* or *divorcé* no longer crushes or withers
one socially, they in their envy of freedom
strike a pace themselves.   The freedom that
is allowable in the—the—*passée* (there is a new
application for that word) is " indecent," or
at least ruinous to the peace and utter respectability of those whom man has not yet " put
asunder."   I must acknowledge that the freedom and joyousness of the court widow are
more or less demoralizing in their effect on
wives.   So many wives cannot understand the
fine sense of honor due to a man whose name
they bear nor the sacredness of even a bad
husband's highest respect.

.   .   .   .   .   .

And that brings me back to my starting
thought; what I am learning about women.

There seems to be three specialties of the sex:
jealousies, lack of honor and "baby talk"—
of course, with gigantic and most delightful
exceptions. I can't understand that "baby
talk." There appears to be some sort of an
affinity between it and maturity. It is generally resorted to by women in the thirties.
Over-the Grass said once, "It is a sure sign of
passing youth, waning attractions and yearning in a woman, whose greatest ambition has
been and is to influence the animal nature in
a man." If I remember correctly, he put it a
little stronger than that. That is strong
enough, however, to apply to my observation
and study of the sex as far as I have gone.
Men must like it, or why under the sun do
these "old girls," women with experience,
women with pasts and women without 'em,
resort to it?

.   .   .   .   .   .

But baby talk is only a trifle. It is the
lack of honor in women that is the most surprising—and yet not surprising. It was the
thought of it that opened up such a flood of
"another part of it" the other night when I
was thinking out their jealousies of each
other. Women have no fine sense of honor,

because they are such awful cowards morally—
timid, sweetly timid, sounds very much better,
but the lack of honor is a mixture of intense
selfishness and abject cowardice. Nature
planned it, so it must be all right. Nature
intended women to be guided and protected
by men, and endowed men with the physical
strength and the moral courage that goes with
it. A woman, instead of having the moral
courage of a conviction, or the bravery to
confess a fault, wins all sympathies, all arguments, all forgiveness, all everything, with
tears. How much could a man win with
tears ?

.   .   .   .   .   .

I believe there are socially three distinct
classes of women—I will have to make four;
there's the good fellow. There is only a few
of her, but—bless her!—she learns honor in
its finest sense from men. Then there is the
wife, the mother, the woman who is tenderly
cared for and who never knows what buffet-
ing against the world means. She keeps
faith and heaven always in sight, and her
sweet mother-face goes with all of us to the
grave. I will place her and the "good
fellow" sacredly away and say there are two

classes of women,—the woman who wants to
progress and be up-to-date in the advance-
ment of women, and the woman who
clings with a drowning grip to youth and
even to the flying tail of Time with baby talk.
The former class expose in clubs and general
society their cowardice and lack of moral
courage, their selfishness, their personal ambitions, by their own would-be adroit wire-
pulling and pushing. The latter class are
clinging and non-committal, and "catty"
and purring, and sweet, pretty, appealing and
successful. With baby talk and tears they
must have attention and love, and they get it.

. . . . . .

Selfishness is the rock that honor in a
woman splits upon. She can be generous to
an extreme, but if she *wants* anything very
badly, she will perjure herself and sacrifice
any friend she has to get it. Honor is an
unknown quantity to her, if her pulse of in-
clination happens to quicken.

. . . . . .

The more I know of women in a general
way the better I like men. And yet, in particular, I love them both dearly. Ah me! I
should think I did!

XXXIII.

Jack, at last! It was a long, weary wait.
Not one word from him, not even a flower,
after he sent Over-the-Grass to me.

.   .   .   .   .   .

Everything went wrong. Even Aunt Tabby
" blew in " for a day before the Lenten season.
Aunt Tabby and slang sound badly in juxta-
position. But most things were bad in Aunt
Tabby's eyes that evening; marble Phyrne,
bronze Bacchante and—*décolleté* me, worst of
all. I wonder what she would have said if
she had found Jack ensconced in the easy chair
in the midst of what she called " cultivated
immodesty?" She would have pronounced
me beyond redemption! But she did not see
him.

.   .   .   .   .   .

How I did *want* to see him; but I would
not send for him. I had told him that
I wanted to see Over-the-Grass once. I
meant once. I could not go into detail of explanation with Jack. If Jack knows me—
loves me—in the way that can make all future

—a future of his and mine—a plane of contentment, comradeship and happiness, there should be a respect for my judgment, without explanation. But men, even men like Jack, cannot give up, at the first impulse, the idea that women are to be petted and guided at all times. Women, to them, are but children.

.   .   .   .   .   .

Men, as a class, make regulations by which women, in whom they are interested, whom they love, must live and breathe. And they wonder why they weary of them! Under their guidance women cease to be entertaining, and they seek elsewhere for associates.

.   .   .   .   .   .

The natural friend of a woman is a man, and *vice versa*. Natural companionship, however, is wrecked if either one—the woman or the man—in their dictation, curb or lessen characteristics, or even bring too much to the surface the atoms that compose the interesting whole. They are two individuals, with individual rights, and the attributes that attract in the beginning of the friendship should not be absorbed by the selfishness or the strong individuality in one or the other. It is fatal to happiness and to a keen interest in each other.

. . . . . .

I wanted Jack to come, but I would not send for him. I waited for him to come to me. Possibly he had been at the time disappointed in me,though he so kindly arranged the meeting between Over-the Grass and myself. Was I, also, to be disappointed in Jack ? I felt if Jack were Jack, as I knew him to be, he would come and he would understand without words. He had not been selfish in not wanting me to see Over-the-Grass; it was for my own sake, as he viewed it. He felt that Over-the-Grass had forfeited all right to come into my presence. He was resenting an insult to me that I appeared too weak to resent for myself.

. . . . . .

One thing there was that Jack could not understand ; some blows are so deep that insult is the most trival part of it all. I had not realized at the time any insult. What was insult ? Nothing. It was, then, two human lives. To be able to feel the insult, at a time when the future is spreading out into horrible black darkness, would be a pettiness that would make one deserving of anything

that might come. Afterward one can realize
tamely that an insult has existed, but it amounts
to so very little. We can think of it, can
speak of it, but when brought face to face with
a question that is again a part of the old life
you do not care for the insult. Others may
resent it for you, but that part is, to you, unimportant. Jack cannot understand this, because he has not lived through such a sorrow
of his own.

.   .   .   .   .   .

No one knows, will ever know, how much
I wanted to send for Jack to come to me, in
these days that I have been waiting. Sometimes I felt that, perhaps, he understood so
little that he would never come again; that
perhaps to him I had been so selfish, so lacking in pride, in principle, that he would never
again be the same to me; that even after
years of friendship and these recent months
of closer companionship, he could not see
clearly *why* I should want to see Over-the-
Grass once more. When these thoughts came
I—walked the floor again. Think of that! I
never thought to do that any more. That cease-
less tramp up and down over the rugs I thought
was a leaf turned down with Over-the-Grass.

.   .   .   .   .   .

I expect that if Jack and I were—were—
well, the ordinary man and woman, I would
have sent for him. We are not ordinary, because we, in the end, never do misunderstand
each other. We fence with words, we have
"edged tools in our tea," we *dare* a great
deal, for the reason that we both know that
'way down in the heart there is a subtle, never-
failing knowledge of each other. If I had
sent for him, and he came because of it, it
would not have satisfied me. If—as I felt
that he did—if he knew his place with me
could never change, he would come in good
time. Though the time seemed so long in
waiting.

.   .   .   .   .   .

And he came. He came in the same old
nonchalant way, and said that he had been
attending to important matters or he would
have come sooner. He ignored the subject
entirely of Over-the-Grass, and of my inter-
views. All the evening there has been a contented, happy gleam in his eyes. It is undoubtedly because—because—I couldn't help running out into the corridor to meet and—it was
the first kiss I had ever given to him. He held
me for an instant as if I would never go again,

and then we were ourselves again—careless and debonair; there was dinner and then coffee and Jack's cigar here in the den.

.   .   .   .   .   .

He was thoughtful. He said only this that was at all personal:

"Child, your greatest charm for me is that you are different from other women." Then he stopped. I was trying to decide whether or no I would encourage him in the discussion of my various proclivities, when he finally knocked the ashes from his cigar and added: "Most women have a habit of proclaiming themselves different from other women, but after you know them well you find them all alike. You are honest to your nature, to your principles. You have suppression, but not deceit. You would in nine cases out of ten be misunderstood, but to know you is to trust you; to understand you is to believe thoroughly in your judgment. I am grateful every minute of my life that I have your confidence."

Jettine brought in the *grand marnier* just then and personalities were dropped. It was a safety-valve for me. My conceit was developing so rapidly that this den would have been too small for me in another five seconds.

XXXIV.

Tom says " it is better to be dangerous than dull."

.   .   .   .   .   .

Tom may be right, but it seems to me that the dullest women are the most dangerous. If a woman is pretty or " artistic " in her make-up—understands all the intricate points and herself—the duller she is the sharper she is—as it were.

.   .   .   .   .   .

There's Belle. *Could* anyone be more dangerous—could anyone be more dumb? Could anyone be more successful in angling? Could *anyone* leave more ruin in her wake?

.   .   .   .   .   .

I think not; her husband ruined financially and morally, his best friend, and incidentally hers—no, *her* best friend, and incidentally his —a pauper, and the world well lost. She is to-day a *divorcée,* but still the same—artistic, appealing, silent.

.   .   .   .   .   .

She is a fair sample of women of this kind. Let me see—Belle must be now about thirty-five. She has, with her beauty and silence, run the gamut of her acquaintance among men of sense and experience, and has now in her train only boys ranging from eighteen to twenty-three. Her rôle is childishness. Years ago, through an indulgent husband who loved beauty and pets, she learned the value of beauty, of silence, of discretion, and of shirking all responsibility. She would not have an opinion—that would make her too old. She would not listen to opinions and arguments among others—she was so young! She never says that, but her looks and manner convince you. Nature helps her out by making her look young, and her childish manners, so shy, so sweet, so silent, do the rest. For years men—men of her kind—men not overstocked with brilliancy themselves, who want women for playthings instead of companions—have vied with each other—vied themselves into ruin for her favor. Why? Because of her beauty in a measure, but more particularly because of her eternal silence. She never under any circumstances commits herself with words —unless it be baby talk, and then it is only a demand to be petted, or a desire to have something that will add to her pleasure.

.   .   .   .

Her discretion is wonderful. It evinces itself not only in her own affairs—she never gossips, or discusses others. She is a sweet, amiable child—of thirty-five—and the rôle is carried out to perfection. She never talks, but she writes. All young girls write reams, you know, but it is here that her discretion is balanced by the other extreme. She pours out her silent soul in innumerable letters— letters to these young boys. Though once she was careless enough to leave on the blotter " Your dear little sweetheart, Trudie " (her middle name is Gertrude), her nearest woman friend and room-mate never once saw an address on one of those letters. Oh, dear, no. She would trust trifling young boys, but not a woman. If she is out with a party of several people, she never leads, but follows. If she should be asked, " What will you have ?" she appeals to some one else in the dearest way with : " What are you going to have ?" I smile at the remembrance of Lalla's answer once when, after a dip in the ocean, the dear little thing appealed to her :

" I ? Oh, I think I will have a milk-punch."

" Do I like that ?" asked the child. There were several gentlemen in the party, and it

was an opportune time for the innocent
rôle.

"I don't know, I'm sure," answered Lalla;
"you taught me to drink it."

It was cruel, but Lalla was tired of playing
mother to the child. Lalla is in the twenties
and Belle in the thirties.

. . . . . .

Belle loves to eat. Drink she does not care
for; it would ruin her beauty. She is a gor-
mandizer and sometimes forgets her part of
the play, or her rôle, in catering to her own
appetite. She does not forget the baby talk,
but overreaches in quantity the amount of
food a child should take. It was amusing the
time Lalla reminded her of it. Belle said so
prettily:

"I want tum more meat, tum more tato,
tum more dwavey."

Alex was silent. Jack looked amused. I
—I wonder how I *did* look? Lalla came to
the rescue in an instant with:

"Well, if you are a woman you can have
it. If you are a child you have had enough."

. . . . . .

Belle is not "one of us" any more. Her
baby rôle was too transparent. Her unselfish-

ness was too cruel and unprincipled. Her beauty even ceased to be a picture after we knew the secrets of the boudoir. Her greediness, her animal nature, wore on the nerves. It took time to discover her—time and women; men never could.

.   .   .   .

A man gives her the benefit of all doubts. He considers her a prize to be won—she is so amiable, so yielding, so innocent, so beautiful. Her beauty is maddening to men, too, because of that eternal silence. They cannot understand her. If she would but talk, *talk*. They would then find her commonplace, irritating, coarse. They do not discover her even after their own ruin should have opened their eyes.

.   .   .   .

She has a smile that is, to them, radiant with soul if they but have the opportunity to develop it. She has eyes that are limpid and a dream of pleasure if they can but see the eyelids droop in languor. Her lips, moist and curved into the pout of a child, seem made for kisses and constantly invite them. If she sighs, they imagine it is for them, or that it is something almost unknown to her child

nature—that her blood is tingling with life
and that it is for them to teach her knowledge.
They never know the moist lips, the dewy,
shadowy eye, the sigh, the baby stare, the red
cheeks, are simply art—the art of the dressing-
table and of the feminine viper.   Her mobile
passiveness arouses all that is fiercest in a
man's nature—as she intends it shall—and her
baby innocence   protects   her against ag-
gressiveness.   Her animal nature makes sin
to her—down deep in her heart—seem as
nothing.

.   .   .   .   .   .

A man for her will sell his soul, sacrifice his
family, his friends, himself, and yet it is never
the love that gives him any peace, comfort or
satisfaction.   He tries to cut loose from her
and cannot.   With one appealing glance he is
her slave again.   He will run from her, far,
far, far, but one written word from her brings
him back again—she gives so few words.   If,
perchance, he does get out of the tendrils of
her fascinations for him, he cannot afterward
dig out of the débris even a friendship for
her.   In the memory of it he has for himself
an intense disgust; for her he has still doubts
and bitterness.

.   .   .   .   .   .

Dangerous? That dull woman, when she understands the art, is a devil. She commences and finishes with men; then invariably, in the thirties, keeps up the rôle with boys. She is a leech, for no man has the heart to tell her what she is and throw her aside, for fear he is making a mistake. She plays her part so well.

XXXV.

Why do I hesitate to marry Jack?

.   .   .   .   .   .

Let me look you over, my dear widow. I think there are several reasons in general and one in particular; you know yourself too well.

.   .   .   .   .   .

You have a curse to love in your make-up. It is individualty. It repels, at times, as much as it attracts. Even Jack, perhaps, would not be satisfied with you—after a time. You cannot be moulded, you cannot be different from what you are, you cannot be controlled excepting through caresses and affection. And Jack might forget.

.   .   .   .   .   .

Jack says, with full knowledge of Under-the-Grass and Over-the-Grass, that you have in the past never loved; that your senses and fancies have been aroused, but not your soul; that with your characteristics love could be as fatal in the wrong hands as it would be heaven in the right hands; that you have not, as yet, known fully that instinct that is born of the

heart without one tithe of passion; that you
must have, yet, the love that will lift you out
and above yourself; that because of this lack
in your life you are yet a child in innocence with all the experiences of the
woman of the world; that were your soul to
be once aroused, it would mean for you a
plunge to hell or to heaven, according to the
circumstances.

.   .   .   .   .   .

And Jack sees, of course, in a marriage with
him, a plunge to heaven for you.

.   .   .   .   .   .

And you? Because you feel that both soul
and senses could be aroused you hesitate the
more. With both so strong in each of you,
one or the other must be the stronger in individuality. Individual action—the will against
better judgment—would be, to an extent,
absorbed. It would be a wretched strain, or
else in the complete absorbing one or the
other would not continue to interest. Wretchedness for one either way.

.   .   .   .   .   .

It is looking a great distance ahead, my dear
self, and you are apparently ignoring all the
happiness that lies in between; but you are

fully aware that the individuality that can make wretchedness can also make the happiness supreme.

. . . . . .

A strong woman's love is the same, in its weakness, as the weak woman's love—both being women. To her, as to the weaker, a smile, a caress, brings sunshine, and a frown clouds. Neglect can break the heart of the strong woman the same as in the weak woman. The present and the future, to her, can look bright or black through love. And yet *love* is not all. It will not kill her mentally, morally, or physically in trouble, neither will it satisfy her entirely in happiness. She cannot for love give up this something that is born in her—this individuality. She must be herself.

. . . . . .

If individuality, by personal magnetism, and in the forgetfulness of love, is drawn from her, she can for a time drift and be contented. If she eventually finds that her strength is being absorbed, and she cannot get away from this magnetism, then she can neither be herself nor the one who so absorbs her.

. . . . . .

The stronger the personal magnetism, the more perfect the soul love, the more individuality in one or the other, or both, is absorbed. Individuality in awakening feels the dragging magnetic chain; it recognizes the helplessness, the impossibility of getting away from it, and wretchedness, a sort of silent, uncomplaining one, comes.

.   .   .   .   .   .

Love, passionate and tender and great, is not all there is in a woman like you, my dear self. You could not be a slave—not even to Jack, the master, for long—and *that* is what, in a measure, was intended by nature.

.   .   .   .   .   .

Every man, be he ever so softened and broadened by intelligence and cultivation, has brute instinct and animal passion. Nature intended him to be a conqueror. His intelligence makes him refined and lenient, but can he be perfectly satisfied for long and know that he is not controlling all there is in the life of the woman whom he loves?

.   .   .   .   .   .

I think not. At first it is her charm. He would not have her less clever. He worships her for it. He trusts her through it. His pride is in her being able to hold her own against him, and incidentally, of course, against all the world. He marries her. He knows her love to be the more sacrificing, her passion the more intense, because of strength and intelligence. He catches a glimpse of perfect submission in her caresses, and gradually comes to feel that he cannot be satisfied until he possesses all. He enters upon the chase with zest and devotion. Through love and experience her characteristics develop and broaden, and as he understands her better he feels her slipping from him. He feels that he is not everything to her. He can grow indifferent, or he can seethe and foam and lash himself into fury, and become wretched and jealous of anything that absorbs her and of which he is not a part. If he cannot be all he is wretched and unhappy.

.   .   .   .   .   .

It is not because he is one whit the less a man. It is because he is a man. Nature made him the protector. How can he protect and not be to her *all* there is in her life?

.   .   .   .   .   .

It is a bad mixture—love and individuality

in a woman. Not one man in ten thousand
would understand; not one woman with
strength could be happy and feel herself in
the chains of love that absorbed all her characteristics.

.   .   .   .   .

You are wise to hesitate, my dear self.
And yet I have no doubt that if you discussed
it with Jack you would find again that the
woman who hesitates is lost.

XXXVI.

Phryne, dear, what would life be without you, and without this den? Your marble ears are just deaf enough, your stony silence just safe enough to receive all my little confidences. I have said so much to you that I could not say to any one else, and here is something more: men and women are great studies, but it is fatal to study beyond surfaces.

. . . . . .

It is fatal to much, but mostly to your own happiness. Do you know, Phryne, that it is much wiser, much holier, to let impulse guide us instead of cold reason? Why should we care for the *reason* of things? Judging things from the surface is often bad enough; why disturb the veneering when the polish is all right?

. . . . . .

Tom says that I do not love Jack, if I can reason; that reason is the last resort of love.

. . . . . .

Phryne, I am going to whisper something into your marble ear—I *do* love Jack, with

all sense and all soul. Indeed I do ; and I
am going to tell him so some day—soon. It
will not be a surprise to him, but maybe it
will satisfy him.

· · · · · ·

Jack is not satisfied. I feel it, I know it,
and yet I am so selfish, and do so enjoy the
play without words. There is a charm about
loving and yet not talking or acting love.
There is a subtle, uncertain sway in this affair
of Jack's and mine that holds me with the
keenest edge of interest. It must be so, too,
with Jack. But Jack is human—probably a
little more so than I—still, Phryne, feminine
blood can run riot the same as masculine blood.

· · · · · ·

It is the perfectly controlled rioting in both
Jack and myself that makes the interest so intense and vivid.

· · · · · ·

Jack's daring and coolness has power that
holds one like iron. He will not discuss personalities, and I know that he will not. I
tantalize him, and he masters me, through this
knowledge. He masters me by his daring,
much more than he knows. Perhaps, though,
he does know.

· · · · · ·

Phryne, dear, and you, dearer unconscious Bacchante, I see the end coming to these hours in the den. If I should marry Jack life would be real again—no more dreaming. There would be no more living my own life. I could not slip away for an hour and shut Jack out. Would I want to? No—not for the sixtieth part of an hour. I would have no life of my own. Reveries, then, would be consumed by companionship.

. . . . . .

It looks as if Jack was not going to wait for me to tell him yes, and that I love him. When he said, " What are you going to do with me, child?" it meant much. When I said, nonchalantly and half-wonderingly, as if I did not know what he meant, " Why, nothing," a determined gleam came into his eyes. He answered as coolly, however:

" Well, I am going to do something with you. I am going to make you my wife in the sight of God, or man, or both—you can arrange it any way you choose."

He never changed attitude or expression.

. . . . . .

Ah, Jack, it is too bad to spoil it all! How can we keep it up if we marry? If we were

man and wife there could be no ring of steel
in this delightful fencing.

.   .   .   .

But the ring in Jack's voice was different
from our ordinary badinage, and instead of
answering him with a ripple of laughter I was
brought up standing. mentally. It was, evidently, an end of trifling with dear old Jack
on this one subject at least. I felt cornered.
I was hot and cold, and in the next ten seconds ran the gamut of emotion. I said finally,
rather lamely, " What shall I arrange?" Jack
took a little easier position, an extra whiff at
his cigar, and it seemed to me that an extra
triumph came into his eyes as he drawled :

" It would be better, considering it from all
sides, that you get in order your ribbons, laces
and fripperies, a traveling outfit, a few invi-
tations to intimate friends, and bid me call
upon a clergyman to make my claim legal."

.   .   .   .   .   .

It surely must come. It is not natural—
after you have had it—to live without companionship. It is all something that is or-
dained by a higher order than we are ourselves. Jack has been grand, unselfish and
patient. I have not made it easier for him.

I have held him outside of so much that is human. This playing with edged tools with word-fencing, this understanding of each other which comes to each through knowledge of all there is in life, is exquisite when there is perfect confidence; but it must have an end.

.   .   .   .   .   .

A woman tests a man's strength when she knows of his honor. Months ago, knowing of all the scars in my heart—Under-the-Grass and Over-the-Grass scars—Jack asked me to marry him. Never yet has he had his answer. I would not say yes, could not say no, and all the time would have been miserable with Jack out of my life. Did Jack know that? Probably. It did not need words.

.   .   .   .   .   .

I wish, Phryne, that Jack was here now. I have a strange foreboding. I want so much to tell him how much I love him. It seems as if I could not, must not wait. Sometimes in the night, in my dreams, I have found Jack gone. Ah, the blankness—just nothing left in life! The suffering was awful, Phryne, when I would first awaken. The impression would be so strong that it would seem as if I

could not wait until morning came to tell Jack
of my love and faith in him, and that I must
feel his arms around me and know that he
is mine. Then morning came, and with it
some of the old memories—that have left the
scars—and I was practical and cold, and could
not give up so easily, could not again try to
find happiness that had before been buried in
so much unhappiness.

. . . . . .

But, Phryne dear, if Jack were here now
I would tell him. How long will it be now
before he returns? He was to be gone three
days. It is only a day and a half. Why am
I so nervous? I never before felt this way.
Could anything happen to Jack? Oh, no. If
anything should happen to King Jack—
Phryne, I have had some sorrows, but could I
bear that? I think not. I will not think of
it. I will be happy. I will give Jack his
answer. I will make him happy. I will devote my life to him. What am I without
Jack? Nothing. Jack is life. How the
hours will drag until he comes!

.

XXXVII.

Only six hours more, Phryne, and Jack will be here!

. . . . . .

In these three days that he has been gone I seem to have discovered a new pain. I did not know there were any untried heartaches for me!

. . . . . .

That would sound like croaking, Phryne dear, to any one who did not know us—would it not? With my reputation for enjoyment and happiness, a place in my heart for actual pain would seem to have been omitted.

. . . . . .

This new pain is a foreboding—a wish that I had told Jack before he left how much I love him! Now that I am going to tell him, the time seems an eternity until he knows. Once or twice since he left a chill has struck across my heart, and the vague half-formed thought has come: What if he should never know? Jack never to know—how could that be! He knows. His heart must tell him, as

mine tells me: but I want to surrender; I
want to be all a woman; I want to tell him
with all the love in my heart, looking through
my eyes.

.   .   .   .   .   .

Ah, Phryne, you are cold—you are marble
—you are—were in life—only beautiful.
Your heart never knew enough of suffering
to enable you to know the full meaning of
love in all its abandon of worship. You took
worship—you did not give it. I—I have
been giving it, Phryne, but it has been en-
crusted with the ice of too much worldliness.
I would not allow myself too much faith and
trust. It is the woman who trusts too much
who suffers too much.

.   .   .   .   .   .

Faith and trust are perfectly safe with Jack.
He *promises* nothing. When a man protests
and promises much, he is on the defensive
with himself; he is building up his own moral
bulwarks as he endeavors to establish your
faith. It is the man who proclaims the least
who gives the most.

.   .   .   .   .   .

Having full knowledge of life, and realizing
the delights of anticipation, I have waited,

waited, waited for the something that was all the time within my grasp; have played with fire and just escaped the burn; have been thirsting and yet was afraid, perhaps, that when once the flame was allowed to burn, love in its fineness would be consumed in the intensity of Jack's nature and mine. Now that I am waiting, willing and anxious to tell Jack without reserve how much of feeling there has been beneath all the sparring of words, comes this strange foreboding. The happiness, the realization seems to be receding, to be slipping away. In these last six hours I am living a whole life.

. . . . . .

The light in this pretty den grows dim. I am foolish to come in here in the daytime. It is a nook meant for mellow evening light. What a grave this den would be if anything should happen to Jack! How *could* anything happen to Jack? How nervous I am!

. . . . . .

Phryne, as I look around this niche, where we have had so many beautiful hours, and feel the loneliness of it with Jack out of town, I must have thought it out, and arranged it all for him; for his quiet after-dinner smoke, for the hours we have chatted, sparred, fenced and trifled. It has been heaven, Phryne! And then the hours for the revery, with your bowed head and sylph-like curves, and sweet Bacchante over there, with her innocent eyes, and the grate-fire and the soft draperies—beautiful, Phryne? Ah! yes.

. . . .

Thinking it over, Phryne, the reveries have been a long dream of Jack. The months have gone by and dreams must end, and life must be more practical, and the den, I presume, must go. It is not big enough for two—unless one is incidental. Jack and I married, neither one would be incidental. Then, too, Phryne, the den—well, with two lives blended into one, in small quarters, satiety might come. The dear little spot would be too small for a smoking-room for Jack and his friends—too large for me alone—too sacred to tender memory to be neglected, and yet—

. . . .

How dim the light is! The twilight is short to-night. Every corner is filled with a menacing shadow.

. . . .

Strange I should be so nervous, now that I

am going to be so happy! And yet, not strange. For so long it seemed as if some fatality hovered over me, and that happiness in marriage was not meant for me. I expected too much loyalty. Society—modern society—laughs at men who are loyal. Men cannot endure to be ridiculed. I have been afraid to trust again. But Jack is different. Women cannot sway him from the line of honor. My heart is light with trust and love. At last I am awakening from all of sorrow's dreams, and I am to know the happiness, the life that brings out all that is best in women!

. . . . . .

How cold and gray the sky is! Those clouds hang like a pall. I do not like this den in these hours of the day. Shall I have a fire in the grate and lamps—or shall I bury myself in the pillows for one more wait—to pass away the time until Jack comes?

. . . . . .

No. I cannot endure the gloom in the den! I must have light and warmth around me. I will ring for Jettine.

. . . . . .

A telegram? Can it be that Jack is detained? I could not bear that patiently. I

cannot see—the light is so bad—I should have
told Jettine about the lights. I will draw
back the draperies from the windows—I cannot wait for lights now. Dear Jack! If you
are not coming to-night, my tears will come.
It will be—what—is—this?—Jack—Jack—
dead? *My* Jack dead?

. . . . . .

I am dreaming again. Why *must* one suffer so in dreams? Is there not enough that
tears the heart-strings in waking life? Why
do I not awaken? Usually in dreams such
agony causes instant awakening. If I would
awaken, how thankful I would be that it is a
dream. It can only be a dream. God would
not send such a sorrow as that to me. I have
had, innocently, all the sorrows that can come
to women from the sins of men; to have this
one come to me would be to make me wonder
what are the punishments for *wicked*
women——

. . . . . .

Ah, Jettine, Jettine! Come to me! Come
to me and waken me! I am dreaming—
dreaming such a horrible dream, and it seems
so real! Will no one come? I *am* dreaming. I *must* be dreaming. And yet, I am

standing. I have clutched in my hand—so tight that my finger-nails cut—this yellow scrap of paper. There are the pillows—the couch. The twilight is here—the gray is growing darker—the night has come—will no one awaken me?

. . . . . .

I must wake, or I will die with this terrible pain in my heart. No heart can stand such agony, even in a dream. Why don't the tears come—it would help a little! I must awaken myself—I will never dare to sleep again——

. . . . . .

Jettine—you at last! Waken me! waken me! I am dreaming, and my heart is breaking—breaking——

. . . . . .

Awake? And it is true?

THE END.

www.ingramcontent.com/pod-product-compliance
Lightning Source LLC
Chambersburg PA
CBHW020105030726
47498CB00006B/1962